BOOTS, BLESSINGS AND BONUS DAUGHTERS

By

Pam Wormington

Copyrights © 2025 Pam Wormington

All rights reserved

This book or any portion thereof may not be reproduced or used in any manner whatsoever without the express written permission of the publisher except for the use of brief quotations in a book review.

Dedication

To my Farmer and Forever Adventure Partner.

I came for love, stayed for the unpredictable, and learned that country life is anything but slow and steady. Thank you for every muddy boot, runaway cow, starry night, and lots of adventures sprinkled in between.

With all my love

Acknowledgments

These stories would never have made it to print without the encouragement of friends and family who believed in me and this journey.

Some of them will hold this book in their hands, while several have since moved on to their heavenly home. Yet even in their absence, their inspiration has played a huge part in bringing these words to life. If these journal entries bring a laugh, a moment of gratitude, or a bit of light to someone navigating life's chaos, then they've fulfilled their God-given purpose, and for that, I'm truly thankful.

Also, Special thanks to T. Nutt Photography & Design for their outstanding work in bringing the visual elements of this book to life. Your creativity and professionalism made all the difference.

Table of Contents

Time to Go 2
A Farmer and His Wife Travel to a Faraway Land 5
She Married the Milkman…. 11
Have You Ever Met a Vet? 14
Retirement 17
You lift me up 20
Lone Ranger and Tonto 23
Terms of Endearment 26
Working For a Living 29
If it aint broke, don't fix it 32
My Life Has Gone to the Dogs 35
Farming Sick Days 40
Your Perception is Your Reality 43
The Dead Sea 45
Kansas or Bust? 48
Hay Fever 52
Noxious or Obnoxious? 56
The Shocking Reality of Life on the Farm 59
Running with the Bulls 62
You're Fired 65
Directionally Challenged 69
Time Management 72
Job Discrimination 75
Hangin' On For 8 Seconds 78
Downsizing and Upgrading 81
Love is in the Air 88
Two broke to be funny 92
You Can't Take it with You 96
Looking for Love in all the wrong places 99
Along for the ride 103
Greetings from Down Under 106
On the Road Again 112

Moving Mountains and Moving Cows 116
Smells like Money 119
Stirring the Pot 122
Birthin' Babies 125
The Mechanic 129
2 Daughters 2 Wedding 2 Weeks 132
Birthin' Babies Part 2 135
The Cows are Out! 138
A Hanging at Wormington Farms 141
It's not over until the yelling stops 144
Pausing for a Plan 147
Baby in the Beans 150
Deep Doo Doo 153
Bigger isn't always Better 157
Taste like Chicken 160
Fishing with my Father 163
Fishing with My Father, Part 2: It's All About the Bling 165
The Final Cast 169
Cruisin' on the Buffalo River 172
Joy to the world, the Lord 175

Prologue

Faith, Farming, and Falling in Love. Our wedding song was not the theme from Green Acres TV show, but it would have been fitting on that beautiful October evening as I walked down the stone tile floor of Thorncrown Chapel, nestled in the Ozark Mountains near Eureka Springs, Arkansas. A Navy brat by birth, I grew up in cities across the United States. I never imagined the businessman of my dreams would wear Wranglers and cowboy boots instead of a suit and loafers. I also never imagined living in small-town USA, where everyone knows your name and wants to change your relationship status—including my future mother-in-law. But God had other plans—and a sense of humor.

Our first date was the beginning of introductions to old pick-ups, barn swings, fresh air and fertilizer, cows and critters, and his greatest treasures—his daughters, Nicole and Kimberly. It wasn't long before I realized I had stepped into something that was completely foreign.

I traded in my career and high heels for parenthood and a pair of rubber boots, a sports car for a 4-wheel-drive jeep, a Daytimer planner for a Farmer's Almanac—and that wasn't all. The learning curve was steep at times, and I picked up a few tricks of the trade along the way. The first: if at first you don't succeed at driving a tractor, there are always more opportunities. The second: if a thousand excuses don't get you out of farm work, bribing your father-in-law with a pie surely will. However, there are times when I give in and work alongside my man, and we always find that fresh air and funny stories make for a good life full of gratitude on the farm.

I hope that as you read my journal, you will take a moment to laugh at your situation and give thanks for the goodness around you.

And he said... You are my wife,

Goodbye, City Life.

Time to Go

Here at Wormington Farms, we strive to live economically—notice I didn't say practically. We have a Hardy wood stove that heats both our home and our water, which is a good thing with two teenage daughters. The catch, though, is that it has to be fed daily. Every year, we promise ourselves we'll get a jump start on the wood supply, but every year, we find ourselves in a panic when the first snow or ice storm hits. That's when we realize we don't have enough wood to get us through the winter. So, we suit up in our winter gear, oil the chainsaw, and head out into the winter wonderland.

It was definitely a winter day, ice, snow, and freezing temps, when we took on the task this particular year. Fortunately, we only had to travel to the next hill on our rolling farm, where a fallen tree needed to be utilized. As Paul Bunyan, aka my husband, was busy cutting wood, I realized I had not gone to the bathroom before leaving the house—not to mention before putting on three layers of clothing: coveralls, coat, hat, gloves, etc. Some things just can't wait, and this nagging problem was not going away. I spied a nice group of trees that would serve as a refuge. I  managed to unlayer and hold my coveralls off the ground with one hand, position my feet against a tree, and hold myself up off the snow with the other hand. It was then that I looked up to see the entire herd of cows watching me.

Relief didn't come as quickly as my dog, Taco. He was extremely glad to see me and showed his affection by licking my cheeks. Yes, those cheeks. There was nothing I could do, my hands were all occupied. My glove was frozen to the ground, my other hand was holding my coveralls, and if I moved my feet, they would surely slide out from under me, sending me tumbling down the hill—exposed.

All I could do was grin and bear it! It was a humbling moment as I managed to regain my composure and get back to stacking wood with Mr. Bunyan, who was oblivious to everything except the hum of the chainsaw.

It's funny how much smarter your parents seem as you get older. During this ordeal, I could practically hear my mother's all-too-familiar words: "I told you to go before you left the house."

MY JOURNAL

What made me laugh today

_____

_____

_____

What am I grateful for

_____

_____

_____

_____

_____

A Farmer and His Wife Travel to a Faraway Land

'Then I heard a voice of the Lord saying, "Whom shall I send? And who will go for us?" And I said, "Here am I. Send me" Isaiah 6:8

Hurricane Matthew in 2016 was the worst disaster since the 2010 earthquake to hit this country of 4th world status; the devastation would last for generations. We had read about missionaries from Just Mercy living not far from us, preparing to travel to Haiti to help. Then we heard about them on the news, and then they were the guest speakers at church. Sometimes God's still small voice has to be repeated for me to hear it. After this third time of hearing their mission, my man turned around to me with tears in his eyes and said, "I think we need to go to Haiti." I responded without hesitation, "OK." And that is when our life began to change.

Fortunately, friends got the same message and were ready to jump on the boat with us. We gathered medical supplies and packed suitcases, and tried to anticipate what our accommodations would be. Pictures showed tin shanties to be the norm in the poorest country in the western hemisphere, no running water, no electricity, and certainly no appliances that make our everyday life convenient. We attempted to learn a few words in French Kreyol, but Bonjour was about the extent of that lesson.

In 2017, we boarded a plane and headed to this dry and thirsty land where the life expectancy is 61 years of age, and the average daily income is about $4.83 if one is lucky enough to have a job. The country declared several religions, but Voodoo is prominent.

Planes, motorbikes, taxis, and tap taps were the modes of transportation. And then there was the wooden sailboat. Oh, how I had anxiety over that, but by the time we traveled across Haiti, smelling the dirty air and breathing in the filth and fear, I was ready to set sail. We loaded our bags on the Just Mercy boat at sunset to travel across the Caribbean Sea to Ile a Vache, a small island off the southwest corner of Haiti, where Bill and Janet have a home. As the sky got dark, I started thinking about James and John and the other fishermen in the Bible. At that time, Bill turned off the little motor. We could hear nothing but the waves slapping the side of the boat and see nothing but stars twinkling overhead. It was dark, and as I thought about the stories of the Bible and how crossing the sea must have been in something similar to what we were traveling, minus the little motor, a peace came over me. I was no longer able to rely on my abilities, and I no longer had any of my daily conveniences, unless you count the Payday bar in my backpack. A peace that says, I am your God and I will take care of you because you were obedient. It was a stillness and a calmness that said, "I'll provide a way." I am finding it hard to find words to describe the emotions. We talked a little bit about life, purpose, and God. Strangely, no one mentioned the absence of life jackets. The motor started back up, and we 'strolled' to the nearest island, where we were met with dugout boats to carry us to shore. What is a dugout boat? Well, it looks very similar to a wooden dough bowl, but big enough to carry a person; I'm quite sure they were not designed to carry a suitcase.

The Montgomery family and Haitian helpers had prepared us a room full of all the amenities...a bed, a mosquito net, and a fan that would run if the generator worked. We shared a room with our friends, the Martins, who follow us on all kinds of adventures and yet still call us friends. The upper room, which was an open room above our concrete room, is where we would gather to eat the daily diet of rice and beans, and fruit if available. This is where the Payday in my backpack comes into play. We would sit at a beautiful wooden table and benches that Bill had made, and have our prayer time and fellowship looking out over the sea. It was not uncommon during this time for a local to show up wanting food or medical care. I might mention none of us had any medical training,

but we suddenly became qualified to do what we could with what we had, with guidance from the Great Physician. A young boy showed up who had boiling water poured over his head and face by his brother. There are no kitchens as we know them on the island. Folks cook over hot coals in a pit. This little boy never shed a tear, but I can tell you I cried for both of us. One afternoon, while walking to our neighbors and sharing a bit of food that we were able to carry on our heads, and talking to them about the hope of Jesus, we saw a boy who had a very large and deep gash in his leg. Surprisingly, he was able to make it to our home base and wait for us to give him medical care. It was his only hope. Insert a long pause here as I reflect on this moment. His leg needed stitches, the closest thing we had to make this pain-free was an ice cube, and without a sound, we did the best we could. He and his mother were so grateful, and we were so heartbroken. No one should have to live in these conditions, but these kind people know no different.

The day came that we had been preparing for, the hike to a mountain village called Janou. Bill found this village on Google Earth one day, full of people attempting to live off the land and what little means that they had. The hurricane had wiped out their gardens, so we packed seeds, food, and supplies and met them at the base of the mountain before we began the long, hot, arduous trek. We spent time just sitting and staring at each other. Remember, we do not speak the same language. We had been told that we would probably be the first white women to ever enter this village. I wasn't sure what that was going to feel or look like. I can honestly say this was harder physically than any 14,000' mountain I've hiked in Colorado. As we would look out over the sea, the beauty amongst the poverty was hard to comprehend. As we rounded the final corner past a concrete platform that once was a church prior to the hurricane, we saw a tin building, and some ladies were hanging a sheet over the entrance. This would be our bathroom, which consisted of a hole in a concrete block shared with the largest roaches I have ever seen. This is where hospitality began, and I began to feel like family despite the color of my skin or the language barrier. I wouldn't say it was a barrier because, for once, I didn't have to worry about saying something stupid. A smile and a touch meant more than any words. My man was a rock star as he took selfies with the children and showed them what they looked like in the camera. Can you imagine not having a mirror in your home that you look at yourself in every day? Something simple about that. They were full of giggles as if they had no idea how difficult life was for them. A hearty dinner was prepared over the coals; I believe it was chicken and probably rice, and we were ready to call it a day. We planned to sleep on the concrete pad where the church once stood in hopes of a cool breeze, but the village pastor insisted we stay in his home. Sleeping bags were rolled out on the floor along with all the creepy crawly critters, and they wanted me and my man to have their bed. We were so humbled as we lay there, and they lay on the dirty concrete floor by us, and we heard them slide plates from under the bed and begin to eat what was left from our meal. It was the longest night, as it rained on us through the rusty tin roof, and we were so hot and dirty, but joy came in the morning as we could hear the pastor and his wife praying and singing in a tune we recognized in the pre-dawn hour. It warmed our souls.

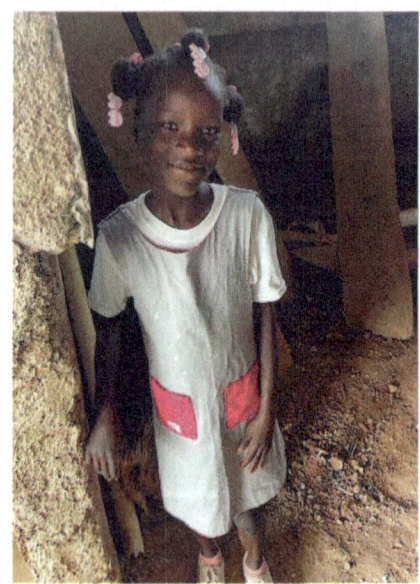

The humor came when a chicken came into our room and walked along the rafter above our bed. It was only a matter of time before the two of us became three. The homeowner snatched it up so quickly, and we began to giggle like little children, under our breath, of course. Hot tea from a rusty can was served with a most generous heart, and we were ready to return to the island via a long hike back down the mountain. Did I mention that I had a guardian angel? Her name is Ermithe. She walked with me, and when I stopped, she stopped. When I was tired, she encouraged me; when I'd slip on the loose rocks, she'd steady me. We couldn't communicate with words, but smiles spoke louder and clearer than anything we could have said.

Back at Ile a Vache via the wooden sailboat, we focused on doing what we could for others and praying for families. I would often ask Bill what the agenda was for the day, and he would just laugh. For people whose biggest concern is where they will find their next meal, they only have one thing on their agenda, and it is easy to prioritize.

In 2019, we returned to Haiti without the Martins but with our new friends, who had been there many times, Michael and BJ. The guys worked diligently on building fish habitats for the sea to ensure the generations to come would have a food source. My new friend, Emily, and I did what we could and observed true happiness when Bill created a job of pouring concrete on the porch that allowed locals to earn a little money. I've never seen anyone so happy to work. I've never seen anyone so hungry. It made us smile as they played music, danced, and laughed while mixing by hand and pouring concrete in the hot sun.

Habitats were rolled into the sea, and once again, we find ourselves on the wooden sailboat. Jumping over the edge to swim in the ocean as the divers secured the man-made reefs to the ocean floor, forgetting that boat ladders and life jackets are not common here.

Amazing friendships were developed, and my best birthday was shared eating a cake and some beverage concoction, and singing under the stars.

Kirk returned to Haiti in 2023; by this time, the gang violence had developed to the point that it was too dangerous for me to accompany him. The guys made a couple of treks to Janou to rebuild the church and love on the locals, providing them with food and a good Word. Concerned about getting home after the airport was closed due to gang violence, learning a new skill of sailing was not on my man's agenda of the top 10 things to learn later in life.

God provided a way, and the guys all made it home safely, but not without a few bumps in the road.

Since then, Dress a Girl Southwest Missouri, another passion of mine, has taken on the project of providing uniforms to these children in Janou who no longer have to walk 2-3 hours down the mountain to school but can attend inside the church building, provided by Just Mercy. Not everyone gets to attend school in Haiti, so this is a privilege, and they get to hear the Lord's promises, too.

My heart breaks for Haiti. These people taught me hospitality means giving what you have with all your heart, even if you don't have much. Our lives will forever be changed by the blessings we received when we stepped out of our comfort zone and into God's plan.

MY JOURNAL

What made me laugh today
_____
_____
_____

What am I grateful for
_____
_____
_____
_____
_____
_____

She Married the Milkman....

Little did she know, the milkman operates just like a United States Postal Service mailman. Rain, snow, sleet, or shine, he picks up and delivers the milk 365 days a year—even on holidays. He doesn't wear a fancy suit or have the latest technology, but you can bet he works tirelessly and stays loyal to his producers and processors. He might not make it home at the same time every day for supper, get to the children's ballgame or school program on time, or even make it to church on Sunday, but you can be sure he tried.

Some days, he might want to quit and trade it all in for a 'simpler' way of life, but then he looks around and remembers that this is the simpler way. It doesn't always make things easy or fun, but at the end of the day, he knows he did a good job and earned an honest wage to provide for his family.

As the third-generation milkman, the title of "Papa" outweighs them all. When these grandsons became fascinated with trucks, horns, and cows, it made it all the better. You see, the fourth generation is all girls, and taking on the responsibility of this business is not their choice.

In the meantime, the fifth generation has become the milkman's tagalong. Before they were big enough to 'haul' milk with Papa Kirk, they learned to make the honking sign with their arm, so when the haulers pulled into the lot at the end of the day, they would honk their horns before parking their trucks.

It's, without a doubt, a pleasure to watch these grandsons follow in their Papa's footsteps—from doing chores to working on trucks. They not only know the trucks but also can identify which hauler is behind the wheel. These boys even have homemade flashcards that help them spot a truck and call it what it is: a Peterbilt, Kenworth, International, or Western Star. Maybe the truck thing is just one of those things that comes naturally for boys. Nonetheless, their interest and enthusiasm have made their Papa's heart grow even bigger.

But all good things must come to an end, and this is true for the milk route that has provided for our family for three generations, starting with Austin Wormington back in the day when milk was hauled in heavy cans on a can truck. In later years, his wife, Helen, drove a milk truck with a bulk tank. The business was then passed down to Tom and Richard Wormington, and then to Tom's sons, Kirk and Jared.

The simplicity of hauling milk to the local processing plant over the years evolved into tanker trucks and long hauls to other states. Small family farms gradually faded away as large corporate dairies became more prevalent in our country. My 'real' job shifted to being self-employed with Wormington Trucking, where I learned bookkeeping, personnel management, and reporting. The pay wasn't what it once was during my career, but the benefits were good enough to allow me to participate in worthwhile projects and still be available for family.

This decision to park the trucks after 40 years didn't come easily, but rather through prayer and planning. We will always be grateful to those folks who made our living a good one. With humble and thankful hearts, we look forward to spending more time with those grandsons, traveling, and seeing how others choose to live.

MY JOURNAL

What made me laugh today

_____

_____

_____

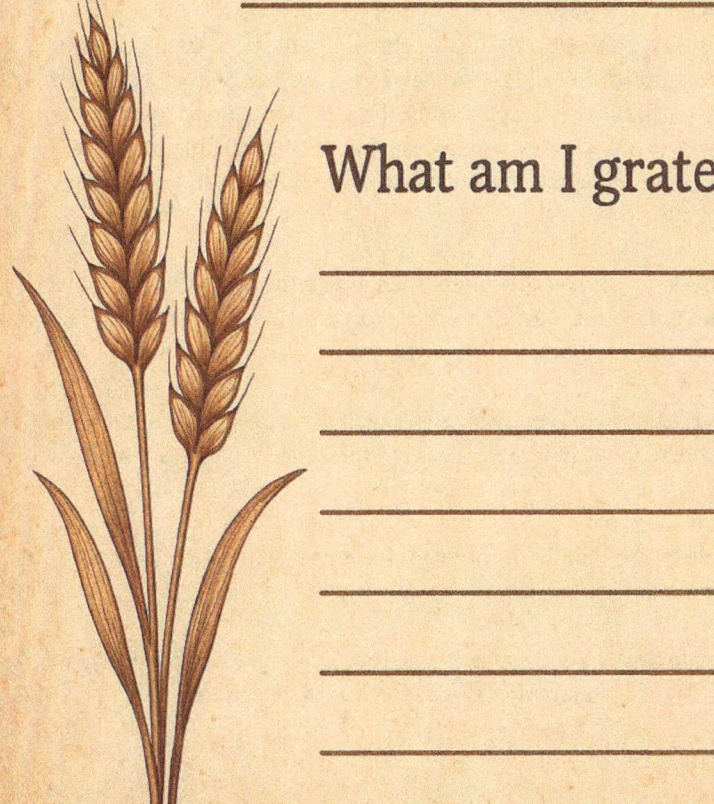

What am I grateful for

_____

_____

_____

_____

_____

_____

Have You Ever Met a Vet?

If you live on a ranch or have a pet, you know that your lifeline is your local vet. Rain, snow, sleet, or shine, they "deliver"—sometimes literally. After 25 years on the farm, I can't even begin to count the times I've called the veterinarian for assistance and advice. I'm a bit embarrassed by what I have learned in some of those moments.

Here are a few of those times.

We typically don't have cattle with horns, but on occasion, we've had a few that needed dehorning. If you've never experienced that, it's like a bloody horror movie. I didn't hear any screeching music, but I could hear my heartbeat as I felt my stomach climb up into my throat. I'm sure the vet was not intending to give medical care to the squeeze chute operator.

My silly Murph, the Labrador, was involved in a traffic accident in front of my house. Thanks to a passerby and a good neighbor, he was scooped up and taken off the road. Who do I call... the vet? She's on vacation but is compassionate enough to calm me and give instructions. She was probably lying on a beach somewhere, soaking up the sun, while I was lying in the front yard next to my dog, tears soaking my cheeks. Thanks, Erin. And thanks, Amber, for telling me the truth, giving me options, and nursing my Lab back to health.

Pregnancy-checking cows—now there's an up-close and personal job. I don't care how long your plastic sleeve is; you are going to get the wrong end of the stick with this job.

And when my little dog, Taco, was dying of old age, it was the vet who brought me chocolate as I sat in the exam room trying to process the news. Thanks, Sam.

Calving trouble in the middle of the night—who are you gonna call? Well, it's not Ghostbusters—it's your vet.

When your male dog is behaving in a way that girls can't comprehend, let your vet explain that 'dominating' desire to you. Thanks, John.

When your miniature mule is sick and you have to make the decision to let her go to greener pastures, who is the one who shoots straight with the facts and the best decision? Who is the one who lets you go inside and ugly cry while he lays her to rest? Thanks again, John.

What's winter weather without calving issues? The rancher calls me while I am preparing supper and asks for help—because that is the designated time, ask any farm wife. I call the vet to tell him that we have a cow with a prolapsed uterus. He asked me a few questions, to which I failed to answer properly, along with my diagnosis, as I was about to burn supper over this discussion. Without completing the sex education class, he arrives and stitches the ole girl up. As I have said many times, "I don't know nothing about birthing no babies." Thanks, John, for explaining the birds and bees—or shall I say, cows and calves—more times than I can count.

The list of stories is too many to remember. We don't call the vet often, but when we do, it's usually memorable. And in case you forget, a bill will soon follow to remind you.

I know it is the cycle of life, but when the boss is away, it seems to spin out of control at times.

When I married my man, I didn't really understand what animal husbandry was—or that it was part of the vows, too.

I've learned that, as tough as the cowboy is, when he loses an animal, it is more than a profit/loss statement. He takes it to heart and thinks he's failed as a good steward. I've learned, as a farm wife, that supper can wait, and so can sleep. When you said 'I DO,' it meant that 'I WILL.' I will do what it takes to take care of what has been entrusted to us.

I'm sure being married to a vet is similar. They are always on call, and even when they aren't, animal health is their heart. Thank you to all the veterinary staff who have helped us make a good life on the farm.

MY JOURNAL

What made me laugh today

_____

_____

_____

_____

What am I grateful for

_____

_____

_____

_____

_____

_____

Retirement

What does that word mean to you? What visions come to mind when you think of that monumental day?

Do you work 9-to-5, Monday through Friday? Maybe you envision a cup of coffee on a leisurely morning as you contemplate what you *want* to do that day. Maybe it means sleeping in on a weekday or staying out late on a weeknight. Maybe it means not doing your hair and makeup or even staying in your pajamas all day.

When I left my "real"—aka paying—job, I thought this would be semi-retirement, kind of like an appetizer to the appealing entrée. I knew the office side of Wormington Trucking would not be full-time. And I knew that filling in the gaps on the farm when the boss was away wouldn't be full-time either.

And yes, I do enjoy a cup of coffee in the morning and am learning to read. By that, I mean learning to stop for a few minutes and enjoy a few pages of a book—because I like the thought that if you're not reading, you're not putting new information into your brain.

But after that, I lose all sense of time management—which, I might add, I have spent years studying and applying. Well, by years, I mean the years prior to marrying a rancher.

For example, today I had coffee, read, and prayed. Then I showered and got dressed—makeup and jewelry—because, well, I will be in public. When I got the call, I need your help sorting cows.

Seriously! I obliged because, well, it is a beautiful day, and I really wanted to go for a walk. I wasn't anticipating carrying a stick and walking behind a herd of pooping cows, stirring up the dust. I might add, when working cattle, I always want to know the plan. I keep getting told there is no plan—this is not something you sit down with the cows and discuss. The plan comes as you go—and sometimes with a loud voice. Today, I asked the same question and got... "I need you to be a fence post." *Insert rolled eyes.* I've always heard old-timers say, "This is just between you and me and the fence post," usually pertaining to gossip. Today, the only thing between him and me and the fence post were some cows that didn't want to cooperate.

After some prayer walking, we were able to get the cows into the corral, sorted, and checked. But there was one who was not happy being isolated and took a liking to the old wooden fence. The fence soon gave way and set her free. Well, not exactly—because just on the other side, there is sometimes a Plan B.

At the end of the day, all ends well, and apologies are accepted for fit-throwing, yelling, attitudes, and actions.

And I am headed to take another shower before heading to the nail salon. I mean, a girl's gotta do what a girl's gotta do.

As we start retirement planning, I wonder what that is going to look like. One day, I asked my man what his goals were for when he gets older, to which he replied, "Haul milk and raise cattle." Ummmm... that's what we do now. Like I said, planning is not something that comes naturally on the farm, so I guess one keeps doing what they love until God leads them in another direction.

MY JOURNAL

What made me laugh today

_____

_____

_____

What am I grateful for

_____

_____

_____

_____

_____

You lift me up

Was it Anne Murray who sang, "You lift me up, up, up to heaven, and you'll never let me down"? Why is it that this song comes to mind when I'm in the tractor and my man is in the bucket? Then, there's always the thought: If you tell me one more time how to operate this tractor using your outside voice, I will show you that I know which handle dumps the bucket. Perhaps I should have thoughts of encouraging words to lift him up instead of physically relying on the big orange tractor. On the ranch, aka farm, there are always dead limbs that need trimming, and what better time than winter, when they can be burned in the Hardy wood stove to heat our home?

It was another one of those days when I had other plans. I drank a couple of glasses of water, skipped breakfast, and threw on my boots and jacket because I was just going to be driving the tractor and only for a few minutes.

I was maneuvering the tractor until I had him lifted up in the bucket and began to gradually accelerate forward and uphill, closer to the tree to be trimmed. At that point, he noticed the tractor was rolling backward. I informed him that my bottom had slid back in the seat and my feet could no longer reach the brake pedal. I think, in a real job, this would fall under reasonable accommodations for an employee. I recalculated and got him positioned where he needed to be, and he transformed into Paul Bunyan with a pole saw—until it became wedged into a large limb. Houston, we have a problem!

The bucket is as high as it will go and the saw is on the end of a pole. After some strategic thinking, I was instructed to get off the tractor and throw up a rope. Safety first, right? The rope would be tied to the pole saw and secured to the tractor to prevent it from crashing to the ground when it becomes dislodged. Then I was instructed to throw a big rock up into the bucket, this would be used along with a wedge to loosen the saw teeth from the limb. I threw the big rock and came nowhere close to the bucket. I threw a smaller rock, it made it to the bucket and struck the larger chainsaw. Optimism says it's a good thing it wasn't the big rock or it could have done some damage. Apparently, that wasn't a good move on my part. I grabbed the big rock again, shored my footing and gave it a whirl with all I had. At that point, I fell backward into the brush pile losing ALL control along with those two glasses of water I drank earlier. I now understand the saying "go big or go home" or better yet "go big and go home," perhaps I should have 'gone before I left home." Good news, he caught the rock and I composed myself after a good laugh and climbed back on the tractor. The saw came loose along with the limb crashing to the ground causing a slight ding in the tractor. Thankful my man was in the bucket and I was in the tractor and not still on the ground.

At that point, I decided it was time for a wardrobe change, so Murph and I, the dog, headed for the house. It's always a good day when you can work together, laugh together, and love life on the ranch.

As I proofread this story to my rancher, I was corrected that one can only be 'in' a tractor if it has a cab; otherwise, they are 'on' it. I'm always 'on' it because I don't have driving clearance to operate anything bigger than the Kubota tractor—something about too much power, too many gears, and buttons. In a real job, that would be classified as unqualified, which is definitely what I am, but sometimes you get what you pay for.

MY JOURNAL

What made me laugh today
_____
_____
_____

What am I grateful for
_____
_____
_____
_____
_____
_____

Lone Ranger and Tonto

Am I right? The Lone Ranger wasn't really alone because he had Tonto. Perhaps this story would have a different ending if I rode a horse, carried a tomahawk, or smoked a peace pipe. Am I right when asked if I can help the rancher catch a sick calf, that it is going to take longer than five minutes and you better change clothes? I already know the answer to the questions. If you are a farm wife, you do, too.

The adorable fall calves were born, but a few had a case of the scours, which we are diligent about catching early and treating. It seems like the calves are not nearly as sick as we think when we attempt to catch them. They can run faster than any ATV, making a roundup in the Ranger a bit like a scene from The Dukes of Hazzard. Let me just tell you that I am a firm believer that if a vehicle was designed with four tires, then they all need to be on the ground at the same time. Apparently, I am alone on the range with that philosophy.

This wet afternoon, I believe it was our anniversary, I got the routine question: "Can you help me doctor a calf? It won't take long, just throw on your rubber boots." In my mind, this means tootling out to the pasture and standing next to the Ranger, handing him the meds while he administers them. Kind of like Nurse Not-So-Goodbody. As my new t-shirt says, "Well, that didn't go as planned." This particular #26 was not only cute but sly and fast. She knew we were looking for her, and she not only hid behind other cows and in the tall grass, but she managed to weave in and out of the herd and zigzag like a squirrel crossing the road. The determination to treat this problem was accelerated by the rancher who heard me scream, "STOP and let me out NOW!" I also don't believe that just because something can go 100 mph, that it needs to. Maybe that is a little exaggerated for an ATV. I am talking about the Polaris Ranger side-by-side. In our younger days, it was a four-wheeler. Fear had overcome me as I thought about the TV show Smokey and the Bandit when meadow muffins began to fly past me. Actually, not all of them flew past me. If you live on a farm, you know grass and water is not an easy mixture to get out of your clothes, and it's not a pleasant aroma on your skin.

I tried to close my eyes and pray, but my faith was not big enough to keep me from wanting to see the accident that I knew I was about to participate.

In my mind, the calf's life wasn't worth more than mine, and clearly, she was outrunning us, so she wasn't as sick as I was at that moment. Now, if you ask the rancher, he would tell you he wasn't driving irrationally or recklessly. Me and #26 have another perspective. And as my friend Cynthia says, "Your perspective is your reality."

Usually, there is a moral to every story, and I am not sure what it is in this situation. Perhaps, when asked the notorious question, I should just say NO, but then what if I got fired? Now there's a thought...

Just like the Lone Ranger needed Tonto, I guess the rancher needs his wife. That's what he tells me, so I will just ride off into the sunset believing that.

MY JOURNAL

What made me laugh today

_____

_____

_____

What am I grateful for

_____

_____

_____

_____

_____

_____

Terms of Endearment

My husband is a man of few words; I think he inherited this trait from his father. He is easygoing, patient, and kind, but when he speaks, just like E.F. Hutton, people listen.

Romancing and sweet-talking are not his thing, so when he exclaims, "Honey, honey, honey!" with the emphasis on the last honey, I know he's talking to me. Like the time I was mowing hay backward, I thought I was all alone and doing a rather productive job until my cell phone rang, and I heard those sweet words, or the time I was driving the big-boy tractor and didn't notice the loader was not up because, well, I didn't see a bucket attached and dug a nice trench in the field. If only I'd had some tulips, I could've made something pretty out of my mistake. This time, those three words were followed up with, "Go get a shovel, and fill in the trench."

I also know that, just like your parent calling you by your entire name, this means I've done something wrong. For example, we were hauling wood from the neighbor's house, and he had just left the premises with a load on the tractor, and I was to bring a load of logs on the pickup. I might tell you that his beloved '97 Ford F250 Diesel flatbed is not my most favorite vehicle to drive. Not just because it is the farm truck and has never seen a good detail job, or the fact that my legs barely reach the floor, or that I can't see over the dash, but apparently, I can't back it either. This is where I would typically insert a grimacing face emoji.

After backing down into a ditch and losing part of my load, I proceeded to put the truck in four-wheel drive and 'make a last-ditch effort' to save myself and what was left of my load of wood. Looking up at the sky—because that's what you see when your truck is at a 45-degree angle—I did what came naturally. When in doubt, give it all you have! I hit the gas, and up over the hill I went. I got out of the truck, rolled the log away that had fallen to the ground, and was attempting round 2 when my darling pulled up behind me on the tractor.

Thinking he'd be proud of how I recovered, I heard those three little words. The same words I have heard multiple times before: "Honey, honey, hoooonneeeeyy!" followed by, "What have you done? There is dirt caked in my receiver hitch?" I had no words. Ironic, I know. That is why I am telling you this story—because I did have words, they just didn't seem necessary at the time.

It's the end of the day, and the wood is at our farm, ready to heat our home this winter. For this, we are thankful, and the truck is in the garage (I didn't put it there), and not another word has been mentioned about my inabilities or skills. Good thing he likes my cooking.

MY JOURNAL

What made me laugh today
_____
_____
_____

What am I grateful for
_____
_____
_____
_____
_____
_____

Working for a Living

I worked in a nice office with controlled heating and air. I got to wear nice clothes, smell good, and was surrounded by others who did the same. I rarely found myself running, sweating, freezing, searching for a big stick, or even wondering why I was there. And then it was time to go home, where the working conditions changed.

It all started when the boss was going to be out of town for a day. He left instructions that any other farmer should have questioned. A fairly new calf wasn't growing as fast as the others, so he thought it wasn't getting enough milk. Perhaps I could take a bottle out to the field and give it a little drink. Oh, the power of milk! Now, I didn't grow up on the farm, but I've been here long enough to know that unless a newborn calf is really sick, a two-legged human is not going to catch it. So, I called my father-in-law, who should have known this, too, but he agreed to come and help. Four legs are better than two, and two brains are better than one — and you know the one I'm referring to. Before we embarked on this adventure, I made the ever-so-wise deduction that if we couldn't catch this calf, it wasn't hungry. As I ran and ran, carrying the bottle, and my father-in-law ran and ran, and the cows ran and ran, and the little calf ran faster and faster, the deduction became factual. At that point, we went to the house with a full bottle.

Today, I was informed that we are weaning our spring calves. We didn't have that on our agenda. He attempted to do it alone unsuccessfully while I was at the paying job in town, and that's when it became part of my agenda, too. Getting cows and calves to the desired location went really smoothly with a lot of prayer walking. You know, walking behind the cows and praying that they don't turn around and decide to go the other direction. It was when the prayer walking became a jog that I slipped on something we like to refer to as a meadow muffin and twisted my ankle. While I complained about my injury, my man separated the cows and calves. He is very good at that, a task that requires patience.

Afterwards, we were surprised to find a little week-old calf that had gotten away from us in the sorting process. As we ran it around three big paddocks, I just had to ask if it was the ONE. Yes, it was the ONE that somebody thought might need a little extra milk because it seemed weak. It was no longer cute at this point, and the game was not fun. The little ONE had run me back and forth along a fence row like I was a cutting horse. Then it proceeded to jump through the fence, and that's when the boss grabbed its back legs and yelled as I grabbed the front, "TACKLE HER! TACKLE HER!" I soon realized that the hold was going to break, so I did just that: laid on it with my whole body. Watching all that Sunday afternoon football during my naptime paid off. I couldn't tell whose heart was beating faster. As the two of us lay on the ground, the boss yelled that a cow was coming back through the gate. "SO," seemed to be all I could manage to say as I held the kicking calf. He ran over and relieved me of the calf, and I ran around the fence to chase the cow back inside the gate. Actually, she stopped and looked at me as if to find it amazing that someone could breathe so hard and expect to be intimidating to a big cow. She casually went back inside the gate, and when I returned, the farmer and the calf were sitting on the 4-wheeler. Ok, I know what you're thinking...who was driving? It wasn't like that. My man had picked up the baby, and they were sitting on the rear rack backwards. I drove them both to where the cows were located and released the little ONE. The momma cow that had come back through the gate had lost her baby in the weaning exodus as well, so we had to put out an APB. We found it in between the round bales of hay.

The sun is going down, and everything seems to be where it should be now. My ankle feels much better, now that my calf hurts. Ever been kicked by a calf in your calf? Something sounds funny about that. Time to shower, prepare supper, and get ready for work tomorrow.

I'm thankful for both my jobs, paying and nonpaying. It seems like the reward from the nonpaying job sometimes outweighs the compensation from the other. I love working with my husband on the farm and the satisfaction that comes with being a good steward of what we've been blessed.

MY JOURNAL

What made me laugh today

_____

_____

_____

What am I grateful for

_____

_____

_____

_____

_____

_____

If it aint broke, don't fix it

I love that old saying, but I have discovered that there could be an amendment to it. If it ain't broke, don't fix it, but what if it is broke and you don't know it?

Some time ago, I noticed an old homemade wagon in the yard of our neighbor, who was selling his house. I inquired to my 'oh-so-practical' husband, "I wonder if they would want to sell that wagon?" His response was as expected, not in my favor. He said I probably could not afford it and should not give it another thought. Well, that was enough for me to keep on thinking about it and all the fun ways to decorate it for every season.

I called the owner and inquired about the wagon. He told me that someone had already purchased it but hadn't taken possession. So, I called the new owner, and yes, she still wanted it; she just had not been able to get her husband to haul it to its new home. This should have been a red flag. So, life went on.

The boss was out of town on a business trip to North Dakota when my brother-in-law called to inform me that the neighbor had moved and wanted the wagon gone by the weekend. The wheels were turnin'. Knowing what the new owner had paid for the wagon, I did a little research on its

actual worth. I called my father-in-law, who was traveling with my husband at the time, to get his opinion. Once my man discovered the reason for my call, he tried to act like we had a bad connection on the line to drop the call. My brother-in-law and father-in-law both confirmed that the wheels would be worth the price alone. Yes, I had the nerve to involve both of them despite my husband's opinion. So, as the saying goes, if you can't get him to join you, find another route. Ok, I may have that a little mixed up.

I called the wagon owner and told her the landowner was gone and wanted the wagon gone. She graciously told me that I could have it, just mail her a check. So, I did. When my husband returned home, I didn't need to tell him what I had done, just convince him to help me bring it home. Trust me, it wasn't that simple. I had used every minute from the point of purchase to the time he arrived home to contemplate this proposition. We inspected the wagon and quickly realized this wasn't going to be an easy transfer, even though it was just across the highway. And while the wheels were worth the purchase price, it didn't mean they worked. It would require a pickup and a tractor. As we carefully disassembled the wagon, we put the bed on the pickup and hauled the axles home on the forks of the tractor. My loving husband placed the axles in the yard just where I wanted them, and then proceeded to place the wagon bed on the ground in the lot next to the house, positioning it so that when placed on the axles, it would be just how I wanted it. I don't know what happened, but all of a sudden, I heard the sound of wood crumbling, a tractor door slamming, and an unhappy husband yelling something about a piece of junk now being a pile of junk! He quickly wheeled his tractor into the barn and gave a whole new meaning to the Moo Juice EXPRESS as he drove the milk truck out of sight. There I stood silently next to this pile of wagon parts. What else could I do but try to reassemble? So, as I dragged piece by piece over to the axles, I contemplated how I should have paid more attention to how the wagon was disassembled instead of how I was going to decorate it. Shortly after, my brother-in-law drove by and stopped to offer encouragement on the puzzle piecing. I figured he was the first to receive a phone call about the recent events. I continued building until I only had a few pieces left over and then called my father-in-law to come secure the wagon with some screws.

It wasn't long before my sweet husband called to apologize for his behavior. He explained the stress he had been under, and that he was just trying to make me happy when the wagon pushed him over the edge. Well, he needed me to give him a ride home from the milk plant, please. I could tell he was rather surprised when I told him I had reassembled the wagon. Apology accepted with a hug and a kiss, along with one more reminder of his behavior — by printing this story. I'm not saying I was right, just determined.

The wagon now has a new home in our front yard, adorned with flowers and red lanterns. It lived out the rest of its life here on the farm with only one purpose: to prove a point and look pretty.

MY JOURNAL

What made me laugh today
_____
_____
_____

What am I grateful for
_____
_____
_____
_____
_____
_____

My Life Has Gone to the Dogs

It all started with a Taco. A little mutt my man found on the milk route. Every day, he would come home describing this little puppy that looked like the Taco Bell dog. Every day, we'd give him the yea-yea nod and go about our business. Then one day, the mutt appeared on the porch and has been there ever since. Taco is a mixture of a red heeler and a Yorkie. Extremely short legs, pointed little ears, and no idea why he chases cows. He had become MY buddy. He sleeps in a galvanized tub on the porch or just inside the kitchen door on the rug when it is stormy or cold outside. He follows me everywhere I go! During the summer, he will follow me to the hayfield and hang out in whatever field I am raking hay, and then follow me to the next.

At the end of the day, he jumps in the tractor and rides back to the house. Odd thing is, we have never trained him to do anything, and that is what he does best — nothing. He can jump on a round bale or in the bed of a pickup, but don't expect him to roll over or play ball. He can beg for food or lay down on command, but don't expect him to shake your hand. Don't trespass on his property or he'll greet you with a wagging tail and a friendly hello. Taco is considered a watchdog; he watches from the porch, and if he sees anything suspicious, he will bark. This includes ghosts in the night, shadows on the barn, and the movement of black cows and mules after dark. Taco likes to go camping and sleeps under our girl's bed. He even went to school for show and tell. He was the most lovable little dog with a big personality.

Feeling left out, the farmer wanted a man's dog. One that would play, wrestle, scare intruders, and look tough. Being the favorite son-in-law, he received a Boxer dog from my dad. Scooby was his name, a cute dog, not very smart, but manly. Oh, I'm going to get in trouble for that statement. Scooby also made his home on the porch, and if by chance you moved his bed, he would stand at the window and give you a scolding in the most hilarious dog voice — not manly. Cold weather came, and coming in the house was not an option. I felt sorry for him, so I bought him a sweater, a manly sweater, no pink or frills. He loved it, and he looked like an old man. Dressing a hyperactive dog is like putting doll clothes on an octopus. Scooby liked to play and roughhouse, but when he got hurt, he was a big baby. He had a minor foot injury, and so without a straightjacket or sedative, we had to be creative with the medical treatment. The ever-so-creative farmer took a piece of plywood and cut a small hole. He propped the board up against the porch, laid the dog on top of the plywood, and pulled his leg through the hole while Scooby laid on his belly. While I petted and calmed the dog, Dr. Economan checked out the injury from underneath. It was minor and treatable, and Scooby healed just fine. Scooby also liked to go camping, but he liked to visit all the campers and check out their supper menus on the grill. This left many campers grabbing their cute little doggies and heading indoors. Unfortunately, Scooby is no longer with us. We suspect he was in a traffic accident. You know, he was chasing traffic, and someone accidentally hit him.

Then there was Buster, a cute little boxer puppy. Buster was expensive, even though he was free. We brought him home and then started the boxer-making process. To the vet he went to be cropped. Crop his ears, crop his tail, cropped... well, we didn't want any other puppies. He was the most lovable puppy. We wrapped him in a towel and watched television with him in the evening until he fell asleep on our laps. Of course, he looked pitiful with all the bandages on his croppings. By the way, these were not manly croppings. Once the ears were cropped, the vet placed a cardboard cylinder in each ear and taped it to train the ears to stand straight. This process was to be repeated frequently to keep the cylinders and bandages clean. Of course, that would mean an additional vet visit and subsequent bills to be paid. Economan and I are somewhat compatible, and I knew that I could intervene and save us a little money. In a house of three girls, I knew where I could find some cylinder tubes just the right size. Unfortunately, the tubes were pink. I proceeded to tape these applicators inside Buster's ears. It was cute until he would shake his head, and the smaller cylinder located inside the larger one would protrude, making him appear to have antennae. The antennae would retract as soon as he stopped shaking his head. Buster grew up, and everything shaped just like it was intended. One day, I was doing a little gardening when a passerby stopped and informed me that my dog was in the road. Buster, too, was yet another traffic casualty. This broke my heart, and it was at that point we vowed to be a one-dog family. Taco was the dog! That was it, no more!

Taco loves to go for a ride in the back of the mini truck. One day, on the way home from the North Ranch, I was driving when some low limbs brushed the top of the truck. Thinking they were going to get him, he jumped out of the moving vehicle. He yelped, and I came to a screeching stop. Limping, he jumped into the front of the truck with me. I was worried he had broken his leg. The next day, I took him to the vet, only to discover he had a torn ACL. Try explaining that to people who see him limping but never see him do anything but lay on the porch. To this day, he has an occasional limp, depending on who's watching and what kind of attention it might bring.

A few weeks ago, the farmer became concerned about the coyotes that were coming closer to the house, intruders in the machine lot, and decided a tougher-than-Taco dog was needed. Taco is set in his ways now that he's older. He doesn't like to play or share much, just like his companion. I like the simplicity of knowing that whatever I leave on the porch will still be there when I return, and in the same shape and form. I like knowing that I can let Taco inside when it's cold, and he will not venture from the backdoor rug. I like knowing that he will always be here, waiting on the porch. He won't bite our guests or lick them; he just greets them with a friendly hello and is satisfied with a good petting.

As you've noticed in other stories, things don't always go my way. It was announced that we would be "trying out" a black Lab. What does 'trying out' mean? "Well, the owners will bring her by, and if she eats Taco for lunch, we won't keep her." I was taken aback by this proclamation. As you can expect, the owners dropped her off and never returned. We named her Black Betty. Amazingly, she and Taco are somewhat compatible. They both sleep on the porch, not on the same side, of course. They both like the same dog food; I only buy one kind. Taco likes his as a meal, while Betty likes hers with a side of work gloves or tennis shoes. I must say she is the most lovable dog (aren't they all?) I have ever met, although her tail is like a lethal weapon. She likes to jump up and kiss you on the cheek. She is very timid and squeaks when petted. She has discovered that she is big enough to block you from wherever you intend to go until you've petted her and given her the attention she desires. If you spend too much time in your car, upon arriving home, she will push your car door open with her nose until she can crawl in the front seat and give you a proper greeting. She loves to play ball and is learning a few tricks, like Stay and Sit. If she gets in trouble, she will slither off until she thinks the coast is clear. I haven't seen her chase cars yet, so I'm hoping she'll be around for a while.

My man recently made the declaration that he wants to trade dogs. "Betty is a girl dog!" Gee, don't let the name be a giveaway. He wants Taco as his dog now. Taco still doesn't like to play or share, but he can jump in the pickup and go for a ride, just like man's best friend. He'll always come when you call, and you can bet he'll never jump up and kiss you on the cheek unless you are squatting behind a tree.

I noticed a coyote in the backyard, and I am glad to report that Betty and Taco saw to it that it left and never returned.

Since the Betty and Taco combination, we've had another black lab named Murph and a fat little corgi named Sassy.

The dogs on this farm are far from what I would call 'working,' but they serve a purpose, and that is to bring us joy and make sure the porch is protected.

My life may have gone to the dogs, but I can't imagine it any other way.

MY JOURNAL

What made me laugh today

_____
_____
_____

What am I grateful for

_____
_____
_____
_____
_____

Farming Sick Days

It hadn't been two weeks since I had hysterectomy surgery when my boss needed my help on the farm. He had a newborn calf that required tube feeding, and the momma cow was not interested in helping with this assisted-living concept. I was not sure what my role would be other than to sit inside the mini truck and dial 911 if needed, but I conceded to the on-call status, despite the doctor having assigned me to light duty. I showed up to work in what had become the normal recovery attire — comfortable pajamas. I pulled on the coveralls over the pjs and loaded myself into the little truck. Over the hills and through the fields we traveled. Hippity Hoppity, not happy all the way. I held my belly, which was held together with surgical tape and sutures, and I held my breath and dug my heels into the floorboard. Once we were at our destination, my man informed me that he had forgotten I was in the truck. I'm sure it was because, for a change, I was not talking.

He managed to feed the little one, then tagged another calf and noticed a new momma who had female parts protruding on the outside of her body that should have remained on the inside upon birthing the new baby. We had to act fast and get her into the corral and call the vet. Herding a new momma cow and her baby is sometimes similar to herding squirrels; they never go in the same direction at the same time. At one point, my frustrated man jumped out of the moving truck and left me with these fleeting words... "You are going to have to do something." I wanted to scream that I was 'recovering,' but as I pondered the long list of doctor's restrictions, I struggled to figure out what that 'something' was going to be, so I slid behind the steering wheel and drove the mini truck, positioning myself between the momma cow and my man just at the right time. It was breakfast time, and I am quite sure she wanted to eat him. As a team, we managed to get the two down the lane and into the corral. By then, I had resumed my original position in the passenger seat in the holding pattern, one hand on my belly and one on my mouth. It was a bumpy mission, and I was quite sure he had forgotten I was along for the ride once again. I was starting to empathize with the cow and her prolapsed uterus, even though I no longer had one. Eventually, everyone was where they needed to be, and I was sent to the house. The vet was on his way.

There are no sick days on the farm for the farmers or their wives.

MY JOURNAL

What made me laugh today
_____
_____
_____

What am I grateful for
_____
_____
_____
_____
_____

Your Perception is Your Reality

I've eaten a lot of crow in my life, but I refused to eat anything that could lick me first. I'm referring to a beef tongue. As a producer of "Naturally Lean" grass-fed beef, I realize I should have tried and learned how to prepare all cuts of a cow. I've enjoyed several delicacies in my travels, but this just wasn't on my top 10 list of foods to indulge.

One afternoon, my practical husband suggested we cook a beef tongue. I don't know where the "we" came into the story. However, I referenced several recipes on the internet, and all of them made it sound delicious and appealing. Of course, I was reminded that the generations before me used all parts of the animal without waste. Inspired by that, I thawed the tongue and proceeded to prepare it according to the recipe. The house soon filled with an aroma that was anything but appealing. I tried to convince myself that it was all in my head until my farmer husband walked in the door, and with a wrinkled nose, quickly retreated back outside with a loud "What is that smell?" exclamation. I told him I was cooking the tongue like he requested! I peeked under the lid, and the sight was more than I could handle. The sight of this gray blob convinced me that no amount of gravy or ketchup was going to disguise this treat.

The smell got worse, and the appetite lessened when "we" finally gave in and called our friends, the Gassers. They like that kind of stuff: tongue, heart, brains, etc. We told them supper was ready and to come and get it! Their oldest daughter, who is now a successful veterinarian and knows all the animal parts, would be coming by our house soon to pick up the goods. I was all too glad to get that pan off the stove and into someone else's kitchen. I had it all packaged up, along with the recipe and remaining ingredients, and sent them on their way. My practical man yelled from outside to open up all the windows, turn on the fans, and light a candle. The weather was still cold outside, and I was freezing, but I regained some appetite and contemplated Plan B for supper is fish.

It wasn't long before I got a call from our friend Gary, asking how I was planning to prepare this heart. I quickly smarted off that I sent the recipe with his daughter, when I realized he said heart, not tongue. Yes, I had the wrong part, but I had so mentally thought I was overcoming this experiment that I had envisioned it to be what it wasn't. Perception is reality! The reality of the matter is I won't be cooking another one of those — either one — anytime soon.

I was rather embarrassed by this discovery and my inability to successfully try something new. I guess my heart just wasn't in it — well, actually, it was. There's a reason the locker plant labels each package. I've since learned the importance of reading those labels. At the end of the day, I was thankful for another option.

MY JOURNAL

What made me laugh today
_____
_____
_____

What am I grateful for
_____
_____
_____
_____
_____

The Dead Sea

It was one of those mornings when everything felt right in my world. While making my morning cup of coffee, I looked out the kitchen window at the sunshine peeking through the fog and noticed something or someone that didn't belong. I squinted a little harder, then grabbed the binoculars, and sure enough, it was little #304, who always manages to be anywhere on the farm except with his momma. Today, he had somehow ended up in the Dead Sea with the donkeys and the bull. We call it the Dead Sea paddock which is located behind our house because much like the Dead Sea everything likes to flow in but nothing flows out. As I assessed the situation, I called the farm boy, who offered a suggestion. Of course, all farm plans are merely suggestions, as they're subject to change multiple times throughout both the planning and implementation processes.

I contemplated over my cup of coffee and breakfast just how I was going to get this little calf back to his momma. I transformed from pajamas to work clothes, from slippers to rubber boots, and made my way to the Dead Sea. As usual, the calf did not want to come out, the donkeys wanted all my attention, and the bull was kicking and bucking like he had a new friend. Plan C came after I took my man's suggestion, and it failed. I opened the gate to the Dead Sea, stood behind a tree, and loudly tried to make myself sound like a momma cow calling for her baby. You laugh, but it worked. Fortunately, it did not attract the bull. The little one came through the gate, looked around, and I ran in behind it, shut the electric gate, and coaxed him to the fence where he originally crawled under. We both crawled back to the pasture where momma was waiting. They were both glad to be reunited, and I was thankful once again that Jesus heard my prayers.

Murph, my companion, and I returned to the porch, panting and tired. Now, what was it I was going to do today after coffee? Once again, agendas are overrated on the farm. We are on flex time.

MY JOURNAL

What made me laugh today

_____

_____

_____

What am I grateful for

_____

_____

_____

_____

_____

Kansas or Bust?

If you are a city girl and your husband informs you that he just bought a pot trailer, your first thoughts are not about hauling cattle. They are about the police hauling you to jail for something illegal. At least, that was the thought before the legalization of marijuana. I eventually came around to the understanding that it had nothing to do with my first impressions. However, let me tell you about my first impression of this cattle 'pot' trailer.

A little history first: my rancher likes to make things himself in an effort to save money, not taking into account time, muscle aches, stress, problems, or any other immeasurable things. He was already in a tizzy about getting the soon-to-be-calving heifers home from the north ranch, and he knew of a trailer for sale around Baxter Springs, Kansas. He thought he could be resourceful and make a livestock hauler using an old Brigadier truck he already had. I just couldn't see how he would come out ahead on this project, so I encouraged him to consider the trailer for sale. His conservative mind and tired body continued to work on the truck until he finally gave in and made a phone call, and we made a journey to somewhere in Kansas.

The trip was multipurpose, of course. We were going to dinner in Joplin, and surely this place wasn't far, so we'd just swing by and check it out. We drove and drove and drove until we saw a 'local' and asked about a pot trailer for sale. We told him the address, and he pointed us down the road—not the yellow brick road, but rather a dirt road. As we continued to drive, I informed my innocent rancher of a husband that not everybody knows what a pot trailer is, and I wouldn't be surprised if that direction-giving man had just led us on a wild goose chase while calling the authorities to inform them that we were looking for marijuana and driving a silver Nissan with license plates FRM WIF. To prove my point, I called my mother, who lives in Maryland, and asked her what she would do should some stranger pull up in her driveway and ask for directions to a pot trailer for sale. It was the same scenario: get rid of them, run to the house, call the police, and lock the door. Momma knows best! We never did find the trailer for sale. We had crossed two state lines, and I was beginning to think my birthday dinner was going to be at a diner in the middle of nowhere with Dorothy and Toto, but by now, we weren't in Kansas anymore. I was anything but excited. By the way, "pot" is short for potbelly, as in potbelly stove. The front of the trailer is the fifth wheel, and then it dips down so that the remainder allows for livestock to be hauled on two levels.

Several days passed, several hours spent working on the truck, and another phone call to the "pot" owners. Finally, better directions came, so my man made another road trip. That evening, I was informed that we were going to be the 'proud' owners of a big red cattle pot trailer. Did I mention big? Knowing aesthetics are important to me, he informed me several times throughout the evening and the next day that the trailer was big and red and not very pretty, and it was my idea to buy it. Well, yes, it was, and I calmly agreed and suggested we park this purchase on the other side of the barn, alongside all the other things that are not aesthetically pleasing to the eye. He apparently didn't think I understood or heard him and reminded me once more that it was BIG and ugly.

The day came when I got the proverbial, "Can you help me?" question. If you are a rancher's wife, you know that any job worth asking for help is not simple or quick. Don't think you're going to run out while cooking supper to help pull a calf, or in a couple of minutes, unload some hay, and don't think going to pick up a big red pot trailer is going to take just a couple of hours. It was 14 degrees the morning we left Monett in the blue Moo Juice Express milk truck, minus the milk tank, and headed to Kansas via Oklahoma. Did I mention my man hauled milk for a living? We pulled onto the bumpiest of roads in the middle of Nowhere, Kansas, and down a lane to what seemed like where we would find the Wizard...but instead, the big, red cattle pot trailer. It was definitely BIG, so big we could haul the circus in it. I remained in the truck, as a proper wife should, with comments to keep under my breath and a story to write. My rancher man jumped out and gave IT the once-over with a good tire kick before the check-writing, title-exchanging deal. The owner pulled up in his Dodge Ram 2500 flatbed pickup and crawled out. It was then I thought I heard wild west music playing in my ears as I noticed Cowboy Garry wearing Wrangler jeans, boots, a black cowboy hat, a big mustache, and a Carhartt coat. He had it all but the horse. This looked like a photo opportunity to me, but I've learned that farmers/cowboys are biased about their equipment and don't always see things the same way city girls see them. You know the saying, "One man's trash is another man's treasure." So, I stayed where I belonged, wondering why I 'belonged' on this trip anyway.

The transaction was made, and the transport was about to begin. The red and blue umbilical cords were connected from the milk truck to the pot trailer; a few adjustments, and we were NOT on our way. By the way, those umbilical cords are brake lines—we certainly wouldn't want to lose this baby on the interstate. The tires were slipping on the ice, and Cowboy Garry grabbed a big chain from his pickup, then proceeded to back up to the milk truck and pot trailer. I'm thinking this is the makings of a Dodge Ram commercial. Surely, he is not going to try to pull this big truck and trailer. Of course not, he is going to push it! Yep, that's what he did, and it worked! We were finally on our way.

Back at the ranch, we looked for a place to park this big, red cattle pot trailer before weaning it from the milk truck. The deciding factor was which side of the barn sees the least traffic.

I'm not really sure what the moral of this story is or what the title of the Dodge Ram commercial would say. I imagine it would be 'Got milk?' or 'Got pot?'. Maybe I should ask the Wizard the next time we are in Kansas. The pot trailer served several years of purpose on the farm until we let it ease on down the road to new owners.

MY JOURNAL

What made me laugh today
_____
_____
_____

What am I grateful for
_____
_____
_____
_____
_____

Hay Fever

It's that time of year when I get hay fever. I see it as an undiagnosed anxiety about driving farm equipment that I am not qualified to operate, combined with the rise in temperature outside. The prescription is not working well, but I continue to take it every year from my farmer. It's usually interpreted something like this: every morning, as soon as the dew dries, take this tractor and ted the hay in that field, then rake the hay in that field, and don't get the equipment tangled up in the gate or electric fence. The side effects: extreme mood swings, an upset stomach, and a possible farmer's tan.

We weren't married long before I understood the meaning of the phrase "let's make hay while the sun is shining." Being eager to please my new husband, I agreed to drive the Farmall Super H that his grandfather once drove. Maybe I should mention that it had brakes when his grandfather owned it. I also should mention that our farm has 'rolling' hills. You don't have to be a math genius to figure out this equation. I was on the tractor, and it didn't matter that my feet didn't reach the pedals because they had no purpose.  My man was on the wagon behind the tractor with the hay loader attached. As I coasted downhill, I found it unmanageable to make all pieces of equipment turn at the same time in the same direction. The tractor turned, but the hay loader and wagon didn't. It was amazing to watch them climb up on the tractor tires, like escalator stairs. It was also amazing how fast my husband jumped off the wagon. Might I mention he was not impressed? I was starting to understand the claim "farming accident," and the thought was going to be how I was classified in the next issue of the Monett Times newspaper. It didn't matter who or what was to blame. My husband (who asked to remain anonymous in these stories), being the patient person that he is, managed to untangle the mess and expected me to continue the job of loading hay as before. I found it difficult to operate the clutch as my legs were shaking uncontrollably. I don't know if I was more afraid of my boss, the tractor, or the upcoming hill that could cause a reenactment. It wasn't long before my father-in-law showed up to lend a hand. Thank goodness he lent his whole self and asked me to get off the tractor. I was more than glad to obey. My job was then to walk the field alongside the hay loader and make sure the bales were in line. I gladly chalked that up to exercise. The heart rate continued as my husband and his dad would laughingly throw a little snake off the hay wagon in my direction just to see me jump and scream. Snakes are not a laughing matter in my book, dead or alive.

The wagon and loader soon retired to a contraption called the hay monster. It's a little hard to describe, but let me give it a whirl. Picture a long flatbed on top of a truck chassis. Down the middle of the bed is a conveyor chain, and to one side, in the front of the wagon, is a steering wheel, a seat, and a fire extinguisher. A long snoot attaches to the front of the wagon, and the driver steers this contraption around the field, lining up the bales that the monster gobbles up and spits onto the wagon, where a person with great balance and strength stacks the square bales. If you can't picture this thing, just drop by sometime in May, and you will not only be able to hear it, but when you see the smoke, you'll know she is working. Bring your work gloves just in case you want to experience the MONSTER. We are always looking for an extra hand or two.

The hay monster retired, and this old dog learned a new trick: square baling! It's kind of like driving a slow train. There's a tractor, a square baler, a wagon, and a boss on the wagon just waiting for a bale to pop out and be stacked. I tried doing his job, but bucking bales above my head—let's just say, I ain't doin' it. Back to the task at hand, instructions go like this: put the tractor in gear, don't drive too fast, don't drive too slow, watch out for the corners, don't let the PTO run too high, make sure the windrows are even or your hay will be lopsided, don't jackknife the trailer, and don't make bales faster than I can stack them. On top of that, the wife in me is watching her middle-aged husband sweat profusely while doing labor that was intended for young boys. I don't know what a shear pin is, but I know you always keep extras in the toolbox.

I'm married to a very patient man, and I don't know if that is a blessing or a curse. At times, I think he will just fire me and hire someone qualified for the job. Then I remember the saying: you get what you pay for… that's how you get me. In the meantime, I'll grab the sunscreen, Benadryl, and hopefully a hot shower at the end of the day, and as long as the sun is shining, I'll do it all over again tomorrow.

MY JOURNAL

What made me laugh today

_____

_____

_____

_____

What am I grateful for

_____

_____

_____

_____

_____

_____

Noxious or Obnoxious?

Just what is the purpose of a thistle? Is it to make farmers crazy or provide job security for the farmer's wife? As life on the farm evolved, so did my appreciation for this pretty purple flower. My friend, the Ag teacher, once told me that a weed is simply a flower out of place. As I recall from the book of Genesis, we learned that sin separates us from God, and the consequences are felt for generations. Because Adam ate from the tree he was commanded not to eat from, the ground became cursed and will produce thorns and thistles.

With that said, I've often heard my boss say that these thistles are noxious weeds. After spending countless hours trying to eradicate them from our farm, I have come to term them obnoxious. More than once, I've been sent to the north ranch, armed with tools, to rid the land of this monster.

One afternoon, I was driving the mini truck with the sprayer in the back and the wand in my right hand as I drove around the field, spraying every thistle. After several circles, going east to west and north to south, and seeing many of the same-looking plants, I discovered that I was probably missing some and double-dosing others. My clever man gave me the idea to take a square of toilet paper, something I don't leave home without, and lay it on the freshly sprayed plant. This would mark my territory.

One afternoon, I thought I would make a quick run through a paddock and check for the pesky purple plant. Nothing is ever quick on the farm if you think it will be. I was on the four-wheeler, armed with the green-handled loppers and a thistle digger (proper terminology for farm tools isn't a prerequisite for this job). If it had a bloom on it, I would lop the bloom, put it in a bag, and dig up the plant. It was a particularly hot afternoon, and I didn't have any water because it was supposed to be a quick job. As the quick job stretched longer and longer, I grew hotter, more frustrated, and exhausted. Then I realized I had lost my boss's new green-handled loppers in the field of green grass. First of all, who in their right mind would make green-handled tools for cutting green plants? I knew exactly what I had done. I used the loppers, laid them on the back of the four-wheeler, and when I drove off, they fell off. I thought surely I could retrace my tracks and find them. Think about this: you're hot, tired, and dehydrated after riding around and around in a field of nothing but grass and thistles. There was no tracing my tracks. I drove around sitting on the four-wheeler, standing on the four-wheeler, and walking without the four-wheeler to no avail. Finally, I gave up and headed to the house, where I had to admit to my boss that I had lost the loppers; yes, the green-handled loppers, yes, your favorite loppers. I thought for sure I would get fired or, worse yet, have my wages garnished. On a positive note, I knew that someday it would snow or the grass would die, and there we would find the green-handled loppers, and we did.

I must admit, my husband is not what I would call 'gifted.' He doesn't believe in buying a gift just because the holiday recommends it or the wife expects it. One afternoon, he called me and told me he had bought me a gift, and it was a surprise. You can imagine what was running through my mind. Could I wear it? Could I drive it? Does it sparkle? To my surprise, it was none of the above—a nice pair of loppers. My very own, to have and to hold from this day forward, for better or for worse.

And he had the nerve to ask me what I was getting him for Boss's Day this year.

MY JOURNAL

What made me laugh today
_____
_____
_____

What am I grateful for
_____
_____
_____
_____
_____
_____

The Shocking Reality of Life on the Farm

It's just farming until someone gets caught in the electric fence, then it becomes entertainment. Why is it that when you encounter an electric fence up close, it's maddening, but when someone else does, it's hilarious?

As you can safely assume, I've become acquainted with our fence on several occasions. One of those was while I was performing my job as gate boss. Most of our electric fence is made of poly wire or high-tensile permanent fencing. I got out of the tractor to open the galvanized gate and proceeded to chain it to the barbed wire fence when I discovered that not all the electric fence was the same. As I did the Electric Slide and sang my little adult ditty, one that all who have been shocked perform, I turned around to tell my 'boss' what had happened, as if he might not have noticed. To my surprise, I thought he was having a heart attack. He was holding his chest and doubled over in the tractor. Quickly, the party was over, no more dancing or singing, and I clarified for him that it wasn't *that* funny! I might add, as I was reading this story to my darling husband for proofing errors, he began laughing uncontrollably again, and then he finally confessed. He had a little foreshadowing on the farm that day as he predicted I would do exactly as I described and allowed it to happen. He claims that, because of the tractor cab and the noise level, I probably wouldn't have heard his verbal warning in time to prevent the incident. I'd like to say I am touched by his heartfelt confession, but I was even more painfully touched by his lack of communication.

As the saying goes, "What goes around comes around." The farmer is quite sophisticated in dodging the electric poly wire when rotational grazing our beef cattle. He uses a plastic fence post to lift the wire over his head and then drives the four-wheeler underneath. This enables one to travel from pasture to pasture without having to stop and open gates because no one has time for that unless the gate boss is around for the task. But it wasn't until the wire slipped off the plastic post and tapped that little button on the top of one's ball cap, which houses an aluminum conductor, that the light bulb went on and the party began. Then, the farmer began to hear the Electric Slide music, too.

I have to mention this story because it wouldn't be fair to just laugh at the farmer and his wife. Our Stotts City neighbor, Bridger, is sort of a lumberjack-sized feller.

Not really your 'Dancing with the Stars' or 'Name that Tune' kind of guy at a glance. He was moving cows for us one day and opened the hot-wired gate, laying it in the tall grass. He proceeded to go about his business when, all of a sudden, he felt what seemed like an electric eel wrap around his leg. His natural instinct was to swing the metal fence post that he was carrying at the long, wiggly thing. I'm not sure how long this cat-and-mouse game continued before he let go of the metal post and stepped away from the electrified wire, but that is one song and dance I would have paid to see.

Electric fence is used in abundance on our farm and seems to be an obvious boundary for the cattle. The momma cows know not to touch it, and the babies know they can walk under it. But us intelligent humans struggle with the "it's hot, don't touch" concept. Even though we've been told that since we were toddlers, we somehow never learn our boundaries.

Some things we never learn!

MY JOURNAL

What made me laugh today
_____
_____
_____
_____

What am I grateful for
_____
_____
_____
_____
_____
_____

Running with the Bulls

With daughters married and moved away, "childcare" — that's one less excuse to get me out of working cattle. Trust me, when it comes to excuses, I've got them. When it comes to hearing them, my man doesn't!

It was time to work calves, which I don't really mind; they are less intimidating than working with their mommas. But why not throw an excuse or two out there to see if it works?

Boots, gloves, and work clothes are on as we head through the corral to our four-legged future. I announce that the **Pioneer Woman** never has to work cattle; she just stays at the lodge and cooks while her husband rounds 'em up and heads 'em out. To that, I get, "She has a TV show and you don't, shut the gate behind you." Well, in my mind, I wanted to spout off something about not preparing supper tonight since I have to work cattle, but a little divine duct tape prevented that comment.

Obviously, he had never read *How to Win Friends and Influence* People by Dale Carnegie because he was about to tick off his other free hired hand — his father. My man told his father that he didn't need to be in the corral with the calves. Of course, I felt otherwise, because that left me in there alone. His father quickly responded, "Why? Do you think I am too old?" which was immediately followed by, "Where did I leave my stick?"

At this point, I wanted to make a connection between age and forgetfulness but was afraid he might find his stick and show me another use for it other than prodding cattle. Speaking of a cattle prod, it's really nothing more than a long stick to poke or prod cattle with to entice them to go in the direction you desire. It makes me feel bigger, in my 5'2" mind, if I can carry a big stick.

It was a fairly calm event. I sorted the calves, my boss walked the little ones up the chute, and my father-in-law operated the new head gate. I'm thankful for the new gate, as the old one didn't always do the job it was intended to, and the last time I used it, the handle came off in my hand. This was often the task I got 'fired' from and sent to the house.

Separating cattle is not always an easy job. It is not a natural occurrence for two 2-legged people to separate a herd of 4-legged animals that weigh at least four times as much as the out-of-shape humans running around the corral, yelling and breathing heavily. The process usually comes with this familiar phrase: **"Why did you let the bull get past you?"**

Well let me explain... the bull weighs approximately 2,000 pounds and can run twice as fast, hence 2 more legs. I weigh only a small fraction of his weight. He was coming toward me at a high rate of speed, and it was the 'natural' thing to do to let him pass. To this city girl, that all sounded perfectly logical. We purchased a bull from our friend Mark and appropriately named him, Hutch. He was a gentle bull but very intimidating to look at, up close. Now, my father-in-law and all his calming cowboy wisdom would tell me that the bull was not charging me, just wanted past me. Well, according to my misconstrued depth perception, it appeared he was wanting to take me down, but just in case all he wanted was to pass me, then I am willing to accommodate him. I think it was clear to the bull when I tripped over my own rubber boots in the mud and manure and rolled under the fence, that I was willing to work out a deal.

Thinking about the answer to his boldly stated question: Why? Why not? Didn't you marry someone smarter than a girl who would stand in front of a charging bull?

It never fails: the animal that you are wanting to keep in a fenced area attaches itself to the bull during the great escape. These animals are mischievous. They know I am going to let the bull pass, so why not team up and tag along? Isn't it true in the business world, associate yourself with those going places you want to go? 'Hang with the big dogs.' 'Run with the bulls.' 'Walk softly and carry a big stick.' All that sounds good in theory, but at the end of the day, I live with the Rancher, and I no longer climb a career ladder. The only thing I'm climbing these days is a fence.

With all that said, I'll keep working cattle when all excuses fail, and he'll continue to get the help that he pays for. Life on the farm doesn't come with promotions or pay raises, workman's compensation, or sick days, but it comes with the satisfaction at the end of the day knowing that you did the best you could with what you were entrusted and who you were entrusted to, and for that, I'm thankful!

MY JOURNAL

What made me laugh today

_____

_____

_____

What am I grateful for

_____

_____

_____

_____

_____

_____

You're Fired

Those words didn't come from Donald Trump; they came from the husband, the boss, the farmer, the one who has been holding back for 12 years. Okay, so I, the apprentice, asked if I could be fired?

It was one of those normal spring days, cows calving, calves hiding from their bawling mommas, 8 inches of rain, and life on the farm seemed like we should've built an ark rather than bought a tractor. I had been out in the rain for quite some time, and my hair was flat and sticky, my clothes were wet, and my nose was running. I was miserable. I finished his part of the chores and went in the house to do a little laundry and prepare supper. The night before, we had a cow whose calf died. And the ever-so-famous words of my husband's grandfather, "He who has, will lose," came to mind. Although it is always disappointing when you have a loss on the farm, it is inevitable. Our intentions were to graft another calf onto this momma cow. We had twins and had been bottle-feeding one of them. If we could graft it onto the grieving momma cow, this would save us a lot of bottle feedings. Gramps also says, "It is always good to have a spare."

With rain pouring, we head out to the field where momma is mourning the loss of her calf. I had a sudden revelation that when she lost her calf, she lost her mind. She headed straight for me! I'm no rodeo clown; I headed straight for the fence. The mud and rubber boots didn't allow me much traction, and I fell face-down in the path of the electric fence. I missed the fence, and the cow missed me. I managed to get up and noticed a slight smirk on my husband's face, along with the look of, "Why did you let that cow get past you?" Trust me, I know The Look! The answer was obvious to me: she weighs ten times more than I, has two more legs, and might just be hungry. It was clear at this point she had her bluff in on me, and I was of little help trying to round her up. Plan B: Round 'em up, rodeo man went to get the modern-day horsepower, a four-wheeler ATV. I had been replaced!

As Nicole, our young farmhand, states, "When she looks out the window and Dad has the four-wheeler on two wheels, things are not good." Mad momma cow gets in the corral, and as she runs toward the head squeeze, I nervously pull the lever. Unfortunately, I jumped the gun and didn't quite get her head secured. At this point, my legs start shaking just like a dog's whose belly is being scratched. The only difference is mine was not a feel-good situation. When the boss came to my rescue, he pushed on the head squeeze, and she escaped by jumping several fences. Now, he is really unhappy, calling her names and using a few choice words. Not words I would have chosen, and I'm not sure he would have either in the right frame of mind. It's off to get the four-wheeler again, and at this point, he sends me to the house. Just like the dog when he is in trouble. You know the sound, "GET TO THE HOUSE!" Emphasis on the word "house" and long pauses between each word in case you have trouble understanding the command.

I ask Nicole to take over for me and help her dad because I think I've been fired! As we watch the one-man roundup, we notice the four-wheeler come to a sudden stop on the pond bank, where mad momma cow has begun swimming to her safety. I explained to the other farmhand the situation, and she calmly says as she's putting on her rubber boots, "I don't mean to be a chicken, but where is Uncle Jared?" Jared is the bigger little brother of the boss. We call on him anytime there is something we girls can't handle. I'm not saying he gladly comes to our rescue, but we are always glad when he does. Unfortunately, that night he was unavailable.

By this time, the boss had the cow back in the corral. It was beginning to get dark, and everyone was tired, wet, and frustrated. We heated a bottle for the calf, fed little Fred, and called it a night. The wet clothes and boots were piled in the kitchen by the back door, and nestled among them was the little wet dog covered in a bath towel; he never minds being sent to the house.

In the morning, the boss and his brother will try to graft the bottle calf onto the mad momma cow. You guessed it, by noon, I was rehired. No pay raise, no increase in benefits, no worker's compensation, and I was demoted from running the head squeeze.

It has been a month, and mad momma is no longer with us. Well, actually, she is, but in another form, and Fred is still our little bottle calf. I still have my job, and life on the farm goes on.

MY JOURNAL

What made me laugh today
_____
_____
_____

What am I grateful for
_____
_____
_____
_____
_____
_____

Directionally Challenged

I know you think most women are directionally challenged, but why is it that some tractors have GPS systems? Well, I am, and ours doesn't. This summer, my husband, the boss, asked if I could mow hay. Sure, I can mow the yard, and how different could it be? Bigger equipment, faster speeds, more acres, the same grass—well, sort of. Why not? I remember asking, "Is there a particular direction I need to mow?" Sometimes, farmers can be particular about stuff like that. His response was, "There's only one direction possible." So, he checked me out on the tractor and equipment and even made a few rounds of the pasture with me by his side to see if I could pass the test. I passed the verbal test and received my learner's permit. Remember my theory: bigger isn't always better.

The next day, the boss left to haul milk, that's his real job, and I prepared for a day at the North Ranch. Okay, it's his grandfather's century farm in Stotts City. "North Ranch" sounds much more prestigious, and that's what my life is all about. I packed my travel bag (toilet paper, Wet Ones, snacks, water, etc.) and set out on my journey. I made the traditional stop at Massie's Super Stop for one last "restroom" break and a large Diet Coke.

Once at the farm, I checked all the equipment and started mowing. Something didn't seem quite right, so I double-checked in my mind everything we had discussed in the training session, including the 'fact' that there is only one direction to mow. I continued mowing the 60 acres as planned. Things were beginning to flow smoothly, and I was more comfortable with cutting corners when, by mid-afternoon, my cell phone rang. It was the boss! He sometimes checks in on me because he loves me. I noticed, as I answered the phone, that he didn't offer a "hello" or any other cordial greeting. This voice didn't sound normal, but before I could inquire, I heard this LOUD voice, which resembled my husband's, ask what direction I was mowing hay. Something told me he didn't really want a reply of North, South, East, or West, and another voice inside told me he was probably nearby and knew exactly what direction I was mowing. Call that woman's intuition. Then his LOUD voice informed me that I was mowing in the WRONG direction. I tried to remain calm and remind him that he told me there was only one way to This response was, "HONEY, HONEY, HOOONEEEY," which translates to, "I love you, I love you, but you are so stupid." I know I'm fluent in the language of marriage. The strong emphasis on the last "honey" changes its meaning from a word of endearment to a metaphor for a dumb farm wife. He then informed me to turn the tractor around NOW and go in the OTHER direction. Apparently, I was driving on top of the uncut hay, and that was a no-no.

So, there are two ways to mow hay: the wrong way and the right way. I may be just the farmer's wife, but I knew what I was talking about when I asked the question. How inconvenient; now I had to learn all over again how to do the corners and realign my mower. I finally got the hang of it and finished mowing the hay. We met at the end of the day, and you know who had calmed down. I realized I wasn't getting fired, as usual. Fearful of my resignation, he inspected the field and told me it was the nicest backward mowing job he had ever seen. Trying not to diminish the compliment, I had to ask just how many backward mowing jobs he had seen. Just as expected, none! It's the thought that counts. He did inform me that the true test would be how the field looks after the mowing and baling are complete. I think he was actually impressed, but not enough to change his way of mowing in the future.

He so graciously marked on his tractor a diagram of the gears in black Sharpie so I could drive it with more skill. Maybe next year, he'll draw me a compass.

MY JOURNAL

What made me laugh today

_____

_____

_____

What am I grateful for

_____

_____

_____

_____

_____

_____

Time Management

To everything, there is a season and a time, and that time is a gift. I guess that is why it's called the Present. This precious gift was graciously given, and so the boss and I knew that we must use it wisely.

The saying goes, "Behind every successful rancher is a wife who works in town." I believe that to be true, but then there is the family business, and behind that success is a wife who knows when it is time to leave her comfortable job and take on the job with Wormington Trucking. We aren't really sure what that job is yet, but we are figuring it out as we go. Who am I kidding? I don't think I've figured out a thing except:

That the generations before me worked really hard picking up milk in cans and pick-up trucks, versus tractor trailers with pumps and tanks.

That my father-in-law did a lot of paperwork and reporting, which makes the learning curve for my new job pretty high. Let's just say, if I don't get an email or call from MoDOT or the IRS, it's a good day!

That being a Sole Proprietor means you are responsible. There is no one else to blame or pass the buck.

That the boss tries to be fair and honest, and sometimes good deeds don't go unpunished.

That loyal employees are priceless.

That time together as a family and leaving a legacy is important, and that is time well spent.

So, with all that said, I've traded in my "office" job at Scott Regional Technology Center for a role on the family farm and with Wormington Trucking. Several have asked if I would be driving a truck. The answer to that question should be listed above in the things I know...I know that would NOT be profitable!

I've traded in high heels for rubber boots, hairdos for ponytails, dress clothes for jeans and t-shirts, and I've also traded in a schedule for flex time.

9 to 5 means nothing anymore, nor do holidays or weekends. There is no overtime, sick days, or snow days, for that matter. I now, work on a flex schedule…I can work at any time of day or night. But every day counts, and if that means eating lunch and watching Andy Griffith with my husband, then I consider that bonus pay. Cooking for someone who is ill or offering a favor, I consider that time well spent. And making a dream vacation come true for a parent, I'd say that beats any benefits package. So, if taking time to do those things means filing a report or paying bills during the evening news and before jumping into bed, then so be it.

Do I miss planning and following "MY" agenda? More than anyone will ever know. Do I miss having coworkers who don't smell like milk and have grease stains on their clothes? Yes, sir. Do I miss using my skills and talents? No, just finding new ways to use them.

My friend Donna often reminds me, "Don't be so busy making a living that you forget to make a life." I'd say there is a lot of paycheck's worth of wisdom in that challenge.

MY JOURNAL

What made me laugh today
_____
_____
_____

What am I grateful for
_____
_____
_____
_____
_____
_____

Job Discrimination

With the job title of Farm Wife, I find most of my responsibilities discriminatory. I base this on the idea of looking like a woman but thinking like a man. In this story, I would like to cover a few items from my undocumented job description.

When it comes to tractors, I should not only be able to drive one but also know what type it is, how to shift gears, the types of oil, motor sizes, and various other parts, especially for those trips to the implement dealer for repairs. For instance, a trip to pick up gears for a mower conditioner. First, let me preface this by saying that when I hear the word "conditioner," I'm thinking of hair, not hay. Sure enough, I came home with the wrong gears and paid the wrong price. In my defense, my only instruction was to "pick them up."

Planning and Purpose: Working cattle with the boss is always an adventure. I might add, it's not as scenic or peaceful as the hiking adventures in the Colorado Mountains. I understand corralling cow/calf pairs and weaning them. I'll just twitch my nose, cross my arms, nod my head, and twirl around in a circle until my womanhood makes it happen. Of course not, but the businesswoman in me thought this would be a good time for a plan. A, B, or C—any would suit me as long as I knew which one we would follow. I was made aware that there is never a plan, and if there is, it is subject to change during implementation. Usually, communication of this so-called plan is in a most unappealing and loud tone. Not to mention, a vocabulary that one has never had permission to use until now. This was not something I learned while obtaining a degree in Communications.

Pampering: I may be a city girl, but I understand that a cow is a female bovine. But why is it that when she is the recipient of name-calling, it is so harsh? She is squeezed between two panels while a large calf is being pulled from her insides against its and her natural will, and she doesn't want to stand still. What's wrong with some soothing music, calming conversation, and a little aromatherapy? I know it's at times like these that I sure could use some of that.

Multi-tasking: Must be an expectation of a woman, regardless of her job. I can do laundry, make supper, and hold a broken piece of machinery while the boss, aka the mechanic, attempts to repair it. He, on the other hand, can eat supper, make laundry, or tear up equipment—all at the same time. So, I guess it's all a matter of perspective.

Time management: Is another story. "Can you come help me? It will only take 5 minutes." Thirty minutes later, I hear, "While you're here, can you help me with this, too?" This is where the term "blackened" was invented when it comes to cooking. And, "Hey, while you're here, jump up on the tractor and lift me up in the bucket." "But, I just got off work and am wearing a dress and high heels," as if I thought he should notice. I might mention, it can be done, but one must watch those holes in the floor of the tractor. You've heard the saying, "Behind every successful farmer is a wife who works in town," and you've also heard the saying, "A woman's work is never done."

"WE": Is an overrated term on a 'to-do' list. I feel like if I didn't create the list, I shouldn't be responsible for its completion. Feelings will get a girl in trouble.

Driving: It's permissible to swerve off the road if you are rubbernecking at a piece of farm equipment or a freshly harvested field, but you are considered a "crazy woman driver" if you swerve while multitasking—say, adding an item to the grocery list, looking for his sunglasses, or digging for a piece of gum in the bottom of your purse. No one carries gum in their pocket, and any of this causes you to swerve.

Organization: Let me just tell you that the boss decided he wanted to take over the paperwork for the annual beef sales to our customers. He fired himself! Not sure how that works, and I wish I could do that on occasion.

All other duties as assigned: There are no words for this section.

Mind-changing: Oh, how that is associated with a woman. But let me tell you, a day can start out with "I need you to ted hay today" and then turn into "We need to wean calves," and then "Wait, I might need you to rake hay." So, here I am on standby, waiting to see what he wants me to cross off his 'to-do' list. As the old country song goes, "Stand by your man, show the world you love him," and I DO!

MY JOURNAL

What made me laugh today

_____

_____

_____

What am I grateful for

_____

_____

_____

_____

_____

_____

Hangin' On For 8 Seconds

Early on in our marriage, I discovered there was no room for a Day-Timer. The local weather forecast determined the day's agenda. It has taken several years, but I have finally figured out a way to fit farming into my planner. Mother's Day is a time to prepare for hay season, and Father's Day is a good time to start swathing fescue. I'd prefer a little more accuracy, but between weather and machinery breakdowns, this will get me close. Each of these tasks requires a window of time to complete, and I don't think that window is easily opened and closed.

Many summers ago, I felt like I had really been put to the Farm Wife test. I had driven, pulled, hauled, and ridden more pieces of farm equipment than any city girl would imagine. I might add it was a prayer-filled summer, at best. My biggest accomplishment was learning to drive a 'self-propelled swather.' This prehistoric, spider  looking equipment is used for cutting fescue seed. Quite similar to a zero-turn lawnmower, but on a much larger scale.

This particular year, you know who, contracted to swath several hundred acres of fescue. I don't know what he was thinking, except that labor was cheap and profit was good. I was reminded that when I left my career, I agreed to help on the farm. It didn't matter whose farm. So, remembering that a profitable fescue season once afforded me a diamond engagement ring, I thought about it and wondered how hard it could be to drive this weird-looking arthropod around and around a large field of grass. I should have thought about it a bit longer. The boss agreed to make one round with me, which generally ensures I don't get tangled up in a fence row. I had no idea I could do so much wrong in such a short period of time. I wanted to be fired! I wanted my career back, along with the high heels and air-conditioned office. Forget fescue prices and the chance of maybe another diamond.

After a lot of yelling and wheel jerking, I was let loose with the swather. It was a long, hot day, and I was tired, sweaty, and hangry when I discovered what 'hydrostatic' meant. It meant hang on for your life! One sharp turn of the wheel and this arachnid went crazy, spinning around and around out of control. I started having flashbacks to my college days of riding a mechanical bull. Finally, I gained control and finished the field of fescue.

At the end of the day, I met up with the boss, who had no idea what had transpired during the 'day at the office.' As we were ready to take the equipment through an old fence gate and park it for the night, I cautiously approached, then gave it a little gas when it suddenly started swirling again, trying to buck me off. I didn't know what to do, so I just threw up my right arm and yelled, "Yee haw!" Once I thought I had ridden for eight seconds, I regained sanity and control of the swather. I looked over at my husband, who didn't know whether to run or cry. As usual, he bowed his head and just laughed.

I'd like to suggest that the next time you purchase a bag of fescue seed to sow in your yard, contemplate what all went into this bag besides grass seed. Although we still have a few pull-type swathers around, I might add that we no longer custom harvest fescue. Instead, we attend the PBR (Professional Bull Riders). It's easier on the marriage, and some things are better left to the professionals.

MY JOURNAL

What made me laugh today
_____
_____
_____

What am I grateful for
_____
_____
_____
_____
_____
_____

Downsizing and Upgrading

Sometimes we find ourselves overwhelmed by stuff, and these good things get in the way of us experiencing simplicity. Ever wonder if our grandparents craved 'simplicity'? I think it has become a desire for a generation that has too much.

When we sold our milk-hauling business, it was a challenge emotionally and financially. As the third generation, it saddened us that there was no desire to continue the business by the fourth generation. We also realized that the business was not as it was in years past. The milkman was now more of a truck driver, longer hauls, constant schedule changes, hours of paperwork, and regulations. As usual, we had a plan, and as usual, God had a better one. We decided that in five years we would 'retire' and travel and do all the things we didn't have time to do. God provided an opportunity in one year, and we knew it was meant to be. That didn't make it easy, but it made it doable. The transition was smooth, our employees continued to have jobs, we knew the new owner who was already in the business, and God once again took care of all the details. Then, God provided an additional income opportunity by using one of our milk trucks to haul water to pool owners. Who knew this would be such an adventure? Well, God obviously. I admit, I thought it was a good idea but was confident it would be seasonal—Memorial Day to Labor Day, and maybe 10 pools a month in our local area. Here we are, year two, and pool boy and his Water Wagon can hardly keep up with the calls, quotes, and deliveries from April through September.

We continue to seek 'simplicity.' Our next project is to calve once a year in the spring, selling, holding back, and doing a bit of shuffling. Have you ever tried to get a herd of girls to sync their cycles?

The next item on the 'simplify' list was to sell two vehicles: the Jeep and the city-girl car, the Lincoln, and buy a half-ton pickup. Sell the beautiful, big 37-foot fifth wheel RV and buy a small travel trailer that I could pull behind my pickup. It took a while for me to finally come to terms with this because, let's be honest, that's a lot of change in the things that I find comfort in, especially the glamping part. In April, we put all three things up for sale. In our minds, we thought the Jeep would sell first, then we'd keep the car until we found the 'perfect' truck. Well, that didn't happen. We were getting ready to meet some friends for dinner when we received a call from a man wanting the car. He said he'd go to the bank and head our way. So, with curlers in my hair, I went outside and bagged up all my belongings. And off the car went to her new home.

In the meantime, shopping for trucks and campers started consuming our free time and increasing our screen time. There was also a bit of a difference in the definition of what an ideal truck would be and what downsizing an RV would look like. From my perspective, if I were going to drive a truck, it was going to be as comfortable as my Lincoln, so I, having always dreamed of a King Ranch, was shooting for the moon. I figured if I missed, I would fall among the stars with something like a Platinum or a Lariat. Have you ever heard the saying, "She has champagne taste on a beer budget"? I don't know what either one of those cost, but I could relate. As for the RV downsizing—having owned three fifth wheels, I was pretty particular about what I wanted and did not want. I couldn't imagine a camper without a fireplace, as that was something we used all the time. I also envisioned downsizing meaning 37' to 30'. We looked at a number of new RVs that fell close to our budget, but they were so poorly made. BUDGET—did I mention that word? Yes, the sale of the RV, car, and Jeep would ideally equal the cost of a newer, smaller RV and a truck. Some days, this seemed so illogical and unattainable. Did I mention my farmer is frugal? Not in a bad sense of the word, but he is just a believer in not spending what you don't have. There were many times I'd find a truck I liked—looks are everything to a girl, of course—and I would text it to my man, and I'd be met with, "Wrong engine," "Too many miles," "Too much money," "Too old," yada yada yada. There were times I thought I felt like God was testing my patience. The same with the RV search—"Too much money," "Too long," "Too heavy." He, in turn, would send me pictures of something the Clampetts owned or something someone had dragged out of an old barn where critters had camped. To which I exclaimed, "No, no, no!" So, one night, I thought, I'll go along with your wishes for a couple's camper, and I found the Grand Design Imagine, 25'. She was so cute and little, but she fit in the budget, and she was considerably newer than our 2014 Keystone Cougar, and she wasn't far from home. He liked it! Hmmm, I tried to play it cool until he said, "Let's go look at it." And we did—he loved it! I was expecting him to come to the conclusion that I was right and that this was too small a camper, and we needed to return to my original idea. It didn't take long for me to realize this wasn't going to happen. So, I had to start planning a way to get over this prank that backfired. Once he convinced me that, at a different season in life, we could always go back to bigger, I began to see his side of the situation. This camper would be easy to pull, easy to maintain, and easy to get us on the road when time allowed. But I hadn't sold my fifth wheel yet, so we returned home and waited.

I had decided not to stress too much, as I still had a Jeep. Although it wasn't convenient for grocery shopping and other adulting activities, it was good transportation. I also had a camper and had reservations to camp with my dad at Stockton Lake—and I did. I enjoyed my big camper, I enjoyed having everyone over for dinner, and I enjoyed my little oasis at the lake. But while at the lake, I got a call that someone wanted to come look at the camper the day I returned home at 2:00! Pulling into the driveway at 12:30, I scurried to unload laundry, food, and do a little staging. The new owners arrived, liked what they saw, and asked to buy it with all the furnishings and decorations. Their intent was to use it as a guest house at Table Rock Lake for the children who were allergic to cats and needed separate accommodations. We did not share that we had locked our cat in the camper at one point, accidentally. They also wanted to know if we could deliver it that week! Nine years of accumulation—or seven Jeep loads of stuff—came into our dining room from the camper. Who camps with five decks of cards, not including Old Maid, four pie plates (my uncle loves pies at the lake), extra paper products, extra clothes, extra extra, and then enough lawn chairs in the basement to seat everyone in the campground? It all had to come out! We delivered the RV to their beautiful lakefront property, and my truck-driving man used every driving skill he had to maneuver it into their shelter. This tight fit required removing the vent covers. As the new owners and I prayed, the positioning took place, and Mr. and Mrs. were so grateful that they invited us to come stay with them anytime, in the guesthouse, of course.

Now we are down to a Jeep, and what about that cute little camper? I don't see it listed anymore, so I assumed it was sold. Now, I had to rethink this whole prank that was kind of growing on me. We made a phone call and found out it was still available, so we took a little road trip. I was told to go inside and sit, pray, ponder, and decide if I could really do this small of a camper. There was no room for big girl panties in this little rig, but I came to the conclusion that she's the right one because she waited for us. We bought it from this nice couple who probably didn't really want to sell it any more than I really wanted to sell my camper. We brought her home, and into the barn she went. I returned two of the seven loads of camper supplies. I filled every nook and cranny and added a few decorative touches with some things I had around the house and a few little splurges to make her our own.

It wasn't long after that that we received a call, and a couple was coming to look at the Jeep. I wasn't too concerned because I figured we had it overpriced. They came, they liked it, and they would soon return with the money. Once again, with curlers in my hair, I cleaned out the Jeep, putting all my belongings and a nice stash of napkins in a to-go bag.

The downsizing dilemma just got real, as I now have no vehicle... not exactly. I have a choice between a farm truck, an anti-AC Jeep Cherokee, a bicycle, or a donkey. It is midsummer and too hot for the latter three, and the farm truck requires two pillows to make driving safe. After a few days, my father-in-law had pity on me and allowed me to drive his truck. He then got nervous, thinking that since I sold all my vehicles, I might sell his, so he allowed me to drive his car.

The truck hunt was in full force, and I was trying not to be frantic. I was also being very attentive to my patience and knowing that people were right when they said God has something good in store. Let me tell you a little story about how He got involved in the truck hunt, too. We found a very nice truck in Springfield. It drove well, checked all the boxes. It wasn't the moon, but it was among the stars. It was affordable, and we liked it, but there were a few red flags. No clear title, a lien on it from Texas. A truck from Texas—not the best situation. There were a lot of paint chips, but still, it was OK. We made arrangements to buy it and drive it home on a Tuesday. Something about the situation didn't make me feel extremely excited, so I prayed for God's will, and if this wasn't it, that He would intervene and give us clarity. Boy, did He. With cash in hand, we pulled into the parking lot and started noticing all kinds of issues that we missed just a few days prior... large scrape on the fender, bad tires, crack in the passenger window, more paint chips, etc. I felt sure this was the clarity that I had asked for, even though it meant I would be riding in the hot Jeep back home, disappointed. Romeo consoled me by taking me to Chick-fil-A and not even complaining that I ordered a soda instead of the free water. We continued the search, far and near, near and far. We were both getting tired of looking at trucks, but we were too far into this 'downsize and simplify' scenario to stop now. It seemed like time stood still, yet with every place I needed to go, I longed for a vehicle to call my own... one with an umbrella, Kleenex, hand sanitizer, AC, a console with my stuff, and the ability to drive without pillows.

I felt like God was clearly teaching me that convenience doesn't equal need. I had what I needed; I just wanted convenience. This helped me reel in my patience when it started stretching thin.

Summer is a busy season and doesn't lend much time to truck shopping. We took a Thursday off and ventured to Republic, where we met with the car dealer who sold us the Lincoln 9 years ago. We talked a lot with him about trucks, engines, vacations, etc. It was then that he convinced us to stop trying to put a square peg in a round hole and to consider a different engine for the truck search. Feeling certain this would make the hunt easier, we took off to Stillwell, Oklahoma, to look at a truck. It was nice, but it didn't scream 'buy me,' so we didn't. We then ventured to Arkansas, but to no avail. Another day of disappointment, but yet, I couldn't be mad because I was very conscientious that I would not settle for convenience's sake.

Friday morning, over coffee, I thought I'd look once more at the marketplace and then I'd move on with my day. I saw THE truck... At first, I thought this must be a scam, so I sent the ad to my frugal farmer. He just happened to be coming through Aurora (the same town the RV came from), where this truck supposedly was located. Oddly enough, we had looked at this dealer's lot multiple times to no avail. In the meantime, I called the dealer, and they had to do some checking, only to discover that it was a new trade-in. My man made a detour in the Wormington Water wagon and gave it a quick look over, then returned to his hauling and called me, saying that I better get to the dealer, drive the truck, and make an offer. I must say that I was a little apprehensive since I was accustomed to him being by my side to ask all the questions and make the big deals. I drove the truck around town and then into the Catholic church parking lot. I was a bit concerned about the sign that read 'Say 1 Hail Mary.' I didn't know what that was, but figured since I had been talking to God all morning, I was probably in good standing. I liked the truck; it checked all the boxes, and it turned out the moon was closer than I thought. I bought the truck! A King Ranch. I think I'll call him King George (Strait).

The hunt is over, the searches were successful, and we only slightly overspent our budget. Two months of searching for simplicity seemed like a long time, but it sure has made me appreciate what I take for granted when I walk out the door and jump into a vehicle that will take me wherever I want to go comfortably. I might add that the camper doesn't have a fireplace, but settling for massaging and heated recliners seemed to be a good compromise. And well, the truck, it took this farm wife 27 years to agree to driving a truck, but with bells and whistles, I was willing to compromise once again. Simplifying also saved us money, and the bonus is that we have found it easier to go camping with friends for a few days in between farming. That's priceless.

MY JOURNAL

What made me laugh today
_____
_____
_____
_____

What am I grateful for
_____
_____
_____
_____
_____
_____

Love is in the Air

Early on in our marriage, I decided to embrace the farm wife life. I thought I needed my own pet—one who would love me just as I am, hang out with me, miss me, and listen to all my struggles. You know, kind of like a best friend with fur. I thought it was a miniature horse that would satisfy this search, but apparently, small in stature doesn't equate to small in price. Economan wasn't really seeing the need or the profitability in this purchase, but wasn't opposed to the pet idea, so he found me a miniature mule—half the size and half the price.

It was so sweet; Valentine's Day was close, and he took me to a farm and introduced me to this little girl who was about five years old, and love was in the air. We bought her and brought her home. I named her Cupid.

It wasn't long before we understood that what she lacked in altitude, she made up for in attitude. My Romeo asked me never to tell anyone that he paid money for who he unaffectionately referred to as Stupid Cupid. But I loved her. I really think he and she had a power struggle. He thought he was bigger, and she proved she was stronger. She was pretty smart, too.

She would stick her head through the fence, grab a bucket, bite the lid, and shake her head until the lid came off and all the horse treats fell on the ground.

For years, she followed me around, especially if I had food. She and I would lie in the pasture, and I would tell her my troubles. Her big ears would listen with no judgment, and she always had a warm kiss for my cheek. She loved a good brushing, a spritz of fly spray, and a pedicure. Thanks to my friend Laurie, we even painted her hooves with pink glitter. I could tell she felt like a diva, and she loved a good selfie. She wore reindeer ears, bunny ears, and let little kids sit on her back. The key word in that last sentence was 'little.' She was not a fan of adults on her back, but her bucks were little, and if you straightened your legs, you could just stand up and get off. She was a good girl!

Even though she was not able to have little ones of her own, she took on the mothering instinct with any orphan calf that was put in her care. I remember one particular day, she was standing by the fence next to the house and would whinny for me. I would come outside, pet her, and return to my chores inside. She'd begin to whinny again, and thinking that she just missed me, I would go back outside and pet her again. We'd have a little conversation, and then I'd return to my task. This went on several times until I realized I didn't see the little calf she was responsible for. I began to look all over the field and down the lane, and she was right behind me each step of the way. When I got to the gate, I crawled under, and to my surprise, she began to pace back and forth with angst. I opened the gate, and off she trotted to the woods. Shortly, she returned, and the little calf was with her. At that point, the rancher began to see her purpose. She loved hanging out with the yearling calves, especially when they were turned out to green grass. She thought she was a wild mustang, running, kicking, and being with those of the same size, until they were separated, at which time her head would go up, her ears would go back, and she would begin to pace the fence.

After 19 years of roaming our ranch, as with all of us, her hair began to gray, and she didn't kick and buck like she used to. But that didn't change her attitude, her ability to listen, or how much she loved to be loved upon. I recently found her in bad health and unable to carry out the life she loved here on the farm. My heart hurt from the arrow that had been shot through it by Cupid.

After a few days of trying everything I could, including sitting in the dirt, holding her head in my lap, and looking into her big brown eyes, I had to make a decision. I might add that I don't get paid enough to make these kinds of decisions, and when the vet showed up, compassionately got down on our level, ground level, and explained the diagnosis and options, I proved that by stomping off in my rubber boots, proclaiming something along the lines of, "I wish I'd never left my corporate job." I went to the barn to get Cupid's pretty purple lead rope and took her for her last walk down memory lane, leaving her in the hands of the vet.

I think about that saying, "It's better to have loved and lost than to have never loved at all." That doesn't bring much comfort to me right now, but I do think there is some truth to it. If I'd never met Cupid, I wouldn't have these fond and funny memories. I'm certain other pet owners feel the same.

MY JOURNAL

What made me laugh today
_____
_____
_____

What am I grateful for
_____
_____
_____
_____
_____
_____

Two broke to be funny

I love the closeness of our family, but sometimes the togetherness can be a bit too much. A few years ago, my husband was loading some alfalfa bales when a freak accident occurred and broke his right ankle. In the middle of winter, "cabin fever" took on a whole new dimension. With trucks and drivers pulling their loads, the milkman could hardly stay put. It wasn't uncommon for him to secure a plastic bag around his cast and hobble outside in the snow with crutches and coveralls. Due to the kitchen being remodeled, the microwave was now located in our bedroom upstairs, along with a small table and Rubbermaid tubs of dishes and food. I have always loved a good bed and breakfast.

Less than a week later, we were preparing for my birthday party when we got the scary call from our oldest daughter, Nicole, exclaiming that our youngest daughter was in a head-on car accident just outside Aurora. I was amazed at how fast this one-legged daddy could get himself and his cast and crutches in the back of my vehicle. I was equally amazed at how much faster he thought I could drive with his backseat instructions. The 12-mile trip seemed like it was across the state. Thankful for four-wheel drive and a fast-beating heart, I was able to get us there, pass the traffic, and into the ditch next to the wreckage. The ambulance was occupied, and we instructed our son-in-law to take our vehicle and our daughter to the hospital. After all, our vehicle was already 'handicapped' equipped. As I stood there with my husband on crutches and no vehicle, I had another brief moment of panic that screamed, "What now?" Fortunately, a coworker of Kimber's, who had witnessed the accident and had stayed on the scene, offered to take us to our other daughter's vehicle, which was parked on the opposite side of the accident scene. Once we arrived at her car, I proceeded to get out and thank Tia for all her help. She so calmly replied with, "Your husband is lying in the ditch." Apparently, sliding out of the back seat of a high-profile vehicle on a slope is a challenge for a man with one leg and two crutches. He was okay, just a bit of bruised pride.

We were very thankful that our daughter's injuries were no more than a broken right foot and some lacerations. While standing in her hospital room, she made a proclamation that caught me so off guard, I didn't know whether to laugh or cry. "Since I can't work and my leg is in a cast, I think I will just come home and hang out with Dad." Why not? Every household needs two people with two broken bones, two scooters, and too much togetherness.

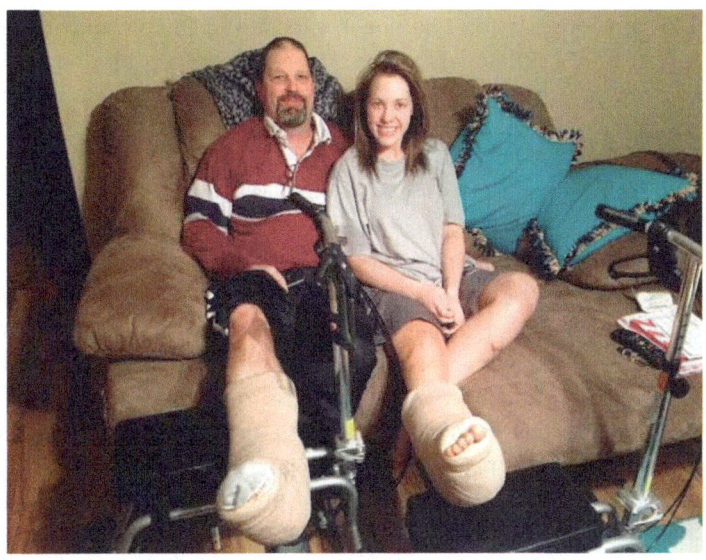

The biggest challenge was getting them home. With both having the right leg casted, that meant the same leg had to be pointed in the same direction while riding in a vehicle with one back seat. This is similar to putting two square pegs in one round hole. Fortunately, once I could squeeze them into the Pathfinder, I could also store their two scooters in the back. I love me a roomy SUV.

After Kimber's surgery, it really hit me that I had too much responsibility. As I assisted my husband and his scooter into the vehicle, the nurse was promptly behind us, wheeling our daughter out for me to take home, too. These two adults were relying totally on me to get them from point A to point B. Of course, with pain meds and some kind of irritable syndrome (my diagnosis, not the doctors'), they managed to find ways to help me improve myself—my driving skills, my conversation, my organization, my first aid skills, my...well, you get the picture. I had hoped that their meds would have made them a bit drowsier. The drive home was long as I thought about different situations and how I would handle them with two handicapped persons in my vehicle, like what if I ran out of gas, or we were in an accident, or the car broke down. Clearly, you know who would be walking for assistance.

Back at the ranch, my man had his chair and stash of snacks and items of necessity, while Kimber had the couch. I might add her spot didn't come with a TV remote like her dad's. This was the first problem of many. Within 24 hours, our daughter had been exposed to Queen concerts and Walton reruns on TV. While I attempted to return to my job and work with the contractor, explaining that the kitchen remodel needed to come to a completion soon, I was continually met with challenges. Yes, my husband and daughter would tattle on each other via text messaging. "Kimber wrecked her scooter," followed by a picture of her lying on the floor, and "Dad went down the stairs to the basement," followed by a picture of an empty scooter next to the stairs. I must confess, I'm not too sure that when I wasn't home, there weren't scooter races in the open kitchen-dining room area and down the hall, but I had no evidence, and as long as there were no additional broken bones, I would just let this be their entertainment. As the saying goes, when life gives you lemons, make lemonade—kind of hard to do when you have no kitchen, but we managed. We took our old cabinets from our 'under construction' kitchen and made ramps so that the scooters and their riders could make it in and out of the house and the den. Also, another speed trap for this daddy-daughter duo who love a good adrenaline rush: the scooter gave them too much freedom if a hill was nearby.

Looking back now, it all seems a blur. He has a new ankle, she has a new foot, and I have a new kitchen.

All is well that ends well, and we have much to be thankful for today.

MY JOURNAL

What made me laugh today
_____
_____
_____

What am I grateful for
_____
_____
_____
_____
_____
_____

You Can't take it with you

The old saying goes in reference to your possessions, "You can't take it with you," meaning when you die. It appears that isn't always the case here on earth. When our kids were little and our friends' kids were little, we thought it would be fun to take them all to a little ski resort in Colorado named Cuchara.

Unfortunately, you can't put that many little ones in one car, unless it's a retired flower car from the local funeral home, and it tows a little U-Haul. Yes, we did! This was also before seatbelts became the safety measure of good parenting. Four adults, a station wagon full of kids, games, snacks, atlas quizzes, and laughs. The U-Haul was full of ski gear and probably tire chains, which I recall we needed. The menfolk were quite proud of their travel arrangements, while us womenfolk just laughed and were thankful we'd see no one we knew. And well, the kids were young, so total humiliation of being seen with their parents wasn't a thing yet.

The long and lonesome winter roads of Colorado can make you a bit nervous, not knowing where the next gas station may be, especially since this wasn't the most economical car in terms of fuel mileage. But togetherness was worth something.

Our condo was perfect for family and friends. Economan's rule was that we hit the slopes as soon as the lifts open and ski all day until the lifts close. Since our bodies are older now, he's a bit more relaxed on that rule, thankfully. I stuffed my girls' coat pockets full of snacks, and Dad carried the CamelBak full of water. Hydration is key while at this altitude, and ski rule #2 is: when you fall, pull out a snack and act like you are taking a break. Our oldest daughter had a not-so-teachable lesson at a Missouri man-made ski resort, so she skis with a more reserved pace, taking in all the sights and moving down the mountain at a slower speed. Our youngest daughter was enrolled in ski school, but due to her hesitation about someone telling her what to do and being born with high-speed determination, she figured out the sport before class. And the reason I adorned her little blonde head with a bright yellow tweety bird cap was for multiple reasons, not only for warmth but so I could spot her as she flew down the slopes. At lunchtime, we'd all meet at the flower car and enjoy 'takeout', take sandwiches out of a cooler, while all those owners of the fancy SUVs with luggage racks in the parking lot sat in the lodge sipping warm beverages and paying for overpriced food. If a picture could paint a thousand words, I can only imagine the gossip.

Tradition is to always have a crockpot of chili waiting at the condo or even hotel after a long day in the snow, followed by hot showers, warm jammies, a crackling fireplace, and kids laughing. This is what truly made our hearts warm.

Good kids, good friends, and good memories, isn't that what vacations are all about? I'd say we came out smelling like a rose on that one. Of course, we did. Look at what we were driving.

MY JOURNAL

What made me laugh today

_____

_____

_____

_____

What am I grateful for

_____

_____

_____

_____

_____

_____

_____

Looking for Love in all the wrong places

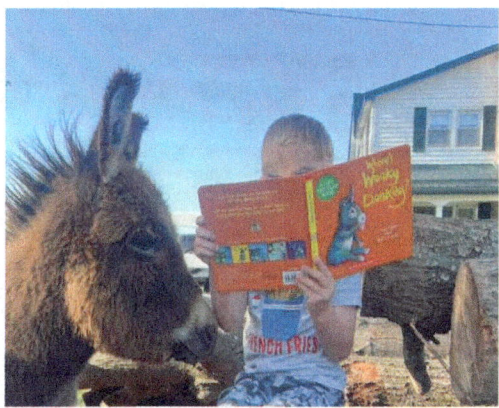

The old-timers used to say that the beauty shop was the place to get in on the latest gossip. This farm wife says it's the best place to find a donkey—a dinky donkey. My hairdresser, friend, and miracle worker, Jennifer, and I visited at the Back Porch for years, and we talked about everything under the sun, from kids, camping, and life chaos, to occasionally crazy farm life. One day, I was telling her about my sweet Cupid, a miniature mule, and how she was nearing the age of greener pastures and that I'd like to bring along another protector of our baby calves and livestock. It was then that she mentioned a sassy girl, Stormy. Stormy is a miniature Jerusalem donkey, and she and her main man, Jack, needed to find a new farm. The price was right, and we were excited to bring the duo home and introduce them to our herd of cattle. It turns out we got 2 ½ donkeys! Hee-haw!

On July 3rd of that year, we 'ooooed and awed' over a little furry girl with big ears and named her Poppy. She was a showstopper—actually, it was the traffic on our farm road that stopped to watch her as she stayed near her momma under the shade tree next to our house. The next year, on July 4th, little 'Sparky' was born, another dinky donkey. At this point, we were really getting a big bang for our buck. Did I mention the 2 donkeys were free? Hee-haw!

Due to the situationship, or as a biologist would call it, inbreeding, Jack and Sparky needed to find new farms and families.

Stormy and her daughter, Poppy, remained here on the farm. They love treats, our grandsons, and scratching their rumps on our white vinyl fence just to hear it snap, crackle, and pop. They are vocal, and it always makes me giggle to hear their braying—especially first thing in the morning to start the day. Unlike Cupid, the only thing I've seen them protect the cattle from is our lazy Lab or the crazy corgi, both of whom are afraid of cows. They do enjoy a rare story time of *The Wonky Donkey*, *The Grinny Granny Donkey*, or *The Dinky Donkey* books, which makes for a fun video to send to your grandsons during a pesky pandemic that leaves us in lockdown.

If you find these two gals adorable, swipe right. Stormy and her daughter, Poppy, watch their figures by eating salad every day, all day, whether it's from the field or my garden, and getting plenty of exercise by power walking the pastures on Wormington Farms. They look identical and are often turning heads of those traveling down the country road. They have great personality, too. However, on occasion, we do have to say the old line, "Don't be an A**!" And it's always funny when the farmer tells me to get my A** out of the corral.

As much as they love us humans, our love, pets, treats, and woes, unfortunately, they are lonely and need a male companion. Actually, they're just looking for a one-night stand. I think, if I bring any more animals to this farm that don't earn us a living, I may get put out to pasture. Do you have a dinky donkey looking for love in all the wrong places? Let's see if we can make fireworks happen. Hee-haw!

Sparks flew when the neighbor allowed his sweet male donkey to come for a farm visit a few winters ago. Unfortunately, it was his last hurrah, as I found him on one cold morning lying in the snow. My man was on a mission trip in a faraway land, and I was beside myself as to what had happened and what I was going to do. My neighbor was very understanding and tried to console me, as this is farm life, and he didn't know how old this jack was or much about his history. His legacy lived on when a cute little Thunder was born. Spunky, attention-seeking, and lovable, he's more ornery than his ears are long.

Once again, we are looking for love. Is there a donkey dating site?

MY JOURNAL

What made me laugh today

_____

_____

_____

What am I grateful for

_____

_____

_____

_____

_____

Along for the ride

I remember my man saying once, "We could have a new house or new cars, but instead, we choose memories, and those memories come in the form of vacations." Recently, on a rainy day, he took my travel journals and jotted down all our adventures over the past 24 years. We were blown away as we reminisced and recollected time with family and friends. There is just no price to put on those things. If there were, this old farmhouse would be a castle, and I'd be the queen.

Whether your escape from 'normalcy' is a good book, a tree stand, or a walk in the park, I think it is important for our mental and spiritual health to look beyond our comfortable routines.

Our journeys have taken us below the sea, snorkeling to mountaintops, hiking Colorado's 14ers, sightseeing on islands and inlands. We've camped in a tent, teepees, and RVs, and stayed in beautiful hotels; we've traveled in Tap Taps in Haiti and vintage automobiles in Romania. We've hiked canyons, ridden horses, cruised on ships and wooden sailboats, fished in lakes, and kayaked in rivers. We've skied on water and in snow. Our kids and their friends have created their own memories together—camping, snacking, and tricking family members with ghost stories and pranks.

As we have gotten older and our kids have grown and set out on their own journeys, our vacations have become a bit more 'extravagant'. Let me explain: I don't mean over the top monetarily, as we still eat sandwiches out of a cooler, picnic in parks, and shop around for deals and steals. By 'extravagant', I mean over the top with adventure and packing in as much as we can into a day. I will say vacationing with 'you know who' is not relaxing, but wow, what a ride! He loves adventure and loves stretching me just beyond my comfort zone in an effort to allow me to see just what is around the corner, or over the hill, or beyond the sea. For that, I am so grateful because God gets the glory when I no longer can rely on my own strength and stamina and get to experience things that are beyond anything man can make.

We have taken a couple of spontaneous vacations, you know, the kind where you know the direction you want to go, but you need a map, GPS, and hopefully a motel at the end of the road. But if not, well, there's a tent in the back seat, and we've got plenty of water and snacks, so no worries. I admit that statement was a little one-sided, and for those who know me, they know which side. I like to think I have a gift for organization, and I also like to use it. I can plan the spontaneity plum out of a trip.

In 2020, determined not to let COVID steal our vacation, we set out in the jeep to journey through Utah. One week and 3,600 miles later, we came sliding into the finish line, breathing heavy and a little scraped up, screaming, "WOW! What a ride!" We camped on the EDGE of Gooseneck State Park overlooking the San Juan River winding through the desert and climbed down into some slot canyons in Escalante. We hiked around Arches National Park, tootled through Dead Horse State Park, Natural Bridges, Canyonlands, and Capitol Reef.

The finish line was Ouray, Colorado, one of our favorite places on earth. Nestled between the mountains, this little town feels like home. So, we took our picnic to the park and lay on the green grass while the sun soaked our faces and dozed off as we gazed at the majestic mountains created by our heavenly maker and celebrated 24 years of marriage, a gift from God. Sure, my future plan was a high-rise in the city, classy clothes, fancy foods, and a career that craved all my time and energy. I am thankful God had a different plan. His GPS is always right on track.

With love,

The Queen

MY JOURNAL

What made me laugh today
_____
_____
_____

What am I grateful for
_____
_____
_____
_____
_____
_____

Greetings from Down Under

A recent trip to New Zealand found the boss and me on an adventure of a lifetime. If the 14-hour flight wasn't enough to exhaust our senses, jumping in a car on the right side and driving on the wrong side of the road in the opposite direction on a roundabout would make one think about the saying, "Don't try this at home."

It was a trip that was three years in the making, and in three weeks, it was over. But those three weeks opened our eyes to unimaginable beauty along the coast of the Tasman Sea on the west, the Pacific Ocean on the east, and the Southern Alps of the north and south islands, with the most gracious people living there in the southern hemisphere, down under. They work hard, and their homes are modest, yet welcoming to family and friends. The cost of living is expensive, with takeaway Fish n' Chips better than a dinner date at Red Lobster. But sometimes, you can't put a price tag on fresh. I was told to eat my weight in Fish n' Chips, and I think I gave it a pretty good shot. The boss made a point to try every kind of meat pie available. Favorites usually got a second chance. Bakeries were strategically placed in most little towns, and spotting and supporting them became a challenge.

Aside from the strong winds across the straight roads of the Canterbury plains, the island roads were extremely curvy. God provided glorious distractions for the passenger in the car. Lush green fields dotted with white balls of fluff that had four legs, large deer farms, alpacas here and there, and an abundance of dairy farms with large milk tankers. Wait, that last one was a distraction to the driver. And that is when I noticed I was leaning in toward the middle of the car to keep us from driving off the cliffs, which did as much good as pushing down on the brake pedal from the passenger seat.

It was nice to do a few touristy treks, like feeding a lamb at the Agrodome while a cute little goat chewed on my hair. Hint to my hairdresser: my hair must look like straw. We floated through the glowworm cave, boated around Milford Sound and watched the itty-bitty penguins and seals sunning on the rocks, paused for pictures at Mirror Lake, and hiked to Franz Josef Glacier but to watch my husband do the Huka, a dance the Maori natives perform was the ultimate entertainment.

We put a lot of miles on our rental car touring both islands, but those are miles I could never adequately describe. Reading a map until there are holes in it is always a good vacation. Laying on a beach looking at the mountains, crystal blue lakes, lighthouses, Antarctica air blowing through your bones (thankful for that Merino wool and possum sweater I splurged on), viewing a volcano, or getting lost and seeing breathtaking waterfalls and rainbows. It's true, not all who wander are lost, but sometimes, lost isn't a bad thing. Our 5-hour drive from one coast to the other lasted about 12 hours. Thankful for our abilities and laughing at our inabilities (like being able to pronounce street signs, reading a map, or following directions from a Kiwi). As the locals say, "She'll be right," meaning whatever is wrong will right itself in time. As my chauffeur says, "We can't get lost on an island, we'll either run into the mountain or the ocean."

Touring milk plants, Fonterra and Open Country, and learning new and innovative ways to make our portion of this industry in America more efficient was interesting—even to this city girl. I don't know that any of our milk trucks will ever haul 29,000 liters a load or have 9 axles, and I'm quite certain we won't be slapping a computer on the side of the truck to test milk at our local dairy barn. We were quite impressed with the operations we visited, and the employees were so friendly. Grassland dairy farms were not quite as frequent as a Walmart or Dollar General in America, but they were a welcoming sight, as we are acquainted with them on a daily basis at home. One man milking 1,200 cows in a rotary-style dairy made me appreciate my easy life and what is on the bottom of my boots.

We skipped the bungee jumping but did visit the original bridge where this crazy sport began. And who could skip the E. Hayes Hardware store in Invercargill, where the Burt Munroe motorcycle story is everywhere? Well, I could have skipped it, but it's not always about me...on this particular day. A curvy road uphill to a castle overlooking Dunedin was breathtaking. Literally! Not sure if it was the beauty or the scary roads. Hokey Pokey ice cream always seemed to calm whatever frazzled nerve I had left with its smooth deliciousness, and not to forget the Whittaker's chocolate that I thought I deserved because it was, after all, my maiden name. As they say, "Good on ya."

Our lodging was wonderful, whether it was at the farmhouse of a friend or in a quaint hotel. There was always fresh milk and a cup of hot tea. The Koru homestay was a bit interesting and an experience we will never forget. The boss will never know that I compensated for staying on a dairy farm with a little luxury in my hotel choices. Sometimes it pays to be the travel agent and accountant. This is where I should insert a winking emoji.

We rounded out the last day of our adventure by digging a hole in the sand at Hot Water Beach and sitting in the hot thermal water, kayaking in the ocean to amazing rock formations at Cathedral Cove, and praying myself through a panic attack as our Tom Cruise look-alike guided me through the cold waves to the calm waters of the Pacific, then prepared hot tea and cocoa on the beach for us. I might add, wetsuits are not warm suits.

Nothing compared to resting my exhausted body in my comfy bed and hearing my husband say, "I've had the time of my life." That will be the closest I ever get to living out a dance scene from Dirty Dancing, and I'm okay with that.

Kia ora

MY JOURNAL

What made me laugh today
_____
_____
_____
_____

What am I grateful for
_____
_____
_____
_____
_____
_____

On the Road Again

Yes, he is a Willie Nelson fan, and he does like traveling. However, traveling with my man on a business trip is anything but the Hyatt, the Hilton, or sometimes even as good as a Super 8. We don't call him Economan just for kicks.

As I've mentioned before, we raise more than "Naturally Lean Beef" at Wormington Farms. Buying and selling used fescue equipment is just another diversification. My boss loves to make trips to North Dakota, South Dakota, and Minnesota, and sometimes even Canada, to check out the swather and combine population.

I would rather travel south, really south. That is where I grew up, and my blood just flows better in warmer weather. I am usually just along for the ride, so we take the northern route.

I recall a particular trip to South Dakota that allowed me to experience the most extreme cold, wind chills of 40 degrees below zero. Yes, tear ducts, nasal mucus, and anything else that runs warm from your body will freeze at this temperature, if outside long enough. We arrived at a farm auction, and I was instructed to stay in the truck and turn the key on periodically to keep the engine warm. I am a multitasker, so I decided to work on a Bible study while waiting in the quiet truck. In the meantime, I had an urgent need that couldn't be met in the cab of the pickup. I bundled up and ventured out into the frigid weather. As I approached the auction site, I realized my husband was dressed just like all the other farmers in brown coveralls, brown Carhart coats, and caps. At this point, I was starting to squirm, and I wasn't about to undress behind a tree. I finally found my man and found the facilities. I was later greeted by the friendliest folks. Inside a building, local ladies were serving lunch to the auction attendees. They soon referred to me as the 'girl from Missouri.' Now that I think about it, I probably did look a little out of place with the continual shivering and teeth chattering. Of all the times, my boss purchases a swather, and that means it must be unassembled before it can be loaded on the trailer. I must tell you, fingers don't work too well in this temperature, and unscrewing bolts and nuts was a challenge. We finally accomplished the task after much whining and complaining on my part. I don't get paid for that added contribution to the work and thought I was just along for the ride.

Another trip entailed loading a piece of equipment from a farmer's house that wasn't home but left his guard dog in charge. I've heard it said a dog is man's best friend, but this dog wasn't friendly. I honestly thought one of us was going to be eaten that day, and I was pretty sure it was going to be him because I was not leaving the safety of the truck. We had been instructed as to where the equipment was located and to proceed with loading it onto our trailer without the owner being present. However, there was one small problem, besides Fido. There was no tractor. A skid steer loader would have to do. If you have never driven one of these, you must know that it is a little tricky. I was laughing at the sight as it reminded me of a student driver... forward, backward, jerk, forward, jerk, backward, jerk. Get the picture? Then picture the big German shepherd running along the outside with my man inside. I finally got out of the truck but perched myself on the trailer with a watchful eye. We managed to get the equipment loaded and left the premises without becoming dog food.

Traveling to Canada was really cool. We spent the night at the Ford Motel. Never heard of it, have you? OK, we slept in the truck just this side of Canada with a blanket, pillow, and the backseat. I purposefully only packed one of each, thinking this would teach Mr. Frugal to get a motel. It only taught me that if I don't want to share, I'd better pack two next time. The next day, we crossed the border and met with the John Deere dealer and a multitude of giant mosquitoes, the national bird. I found the Canadian accent to be quite funny and had to remove myself on occasion from the conversation. Everything was in kilometers, liters, or even Celsius. When I heard on the radio, it was a 'blustery 29 degrees' and it was summertime, I began to wonder if I was back in South Dakota. If you've never filled your fuel tank up with a pump that reads liters, it is a little mind-boggling, not to mention attempting to pay for an ice cream cone and being unable to count the change.

We enjoyed some beautiful countryside, friendly people, and bumpy roads. But the most comforting was the Walmart in Winnipeg. We were informed at the motel desk that one of the world's best beaches was north of Winnipeg. Notice, I said 'motel.' So, we played "Let's make a deal." If I tour the MacDon swather plant, then we can go to the beach. I must say the plant tour was interesting, but the drive to the beach was even more. We drove for miles and miles to what seemed to be a beach closed for the season. The sandy beaches of Lake Winnipeg were pretty, and the boardwalks reminded me of summertime fun at the ocean, but all was quiet except for one or two brave swimmers in the cold waters. It was truly the largest lake I'd ever seen, and the walk along the shore was peaceful.

There have been several other business trips, and with each one comes a few more amenities beyond an ice chest and a backseat. The best accommodations are at the Comfort Inn, or shall I say home, when he chooses to take someone else on a road trip.

MY JOURNAL

What made me laugh today

_____

_____

_____

What am I grateful for

_____

_____

_____

_____

_____

_____

Moving Mountains and Moving Cows

I was looking forward to a weekend of God and girls at a Grounded Faith women's conference in Springfield, followed by a week of camping at the Pines in Arkansas. I planned the work and was executing the plan to get everything done before I left town when I heard the back door open and the dreaded, "We've got a problem!" Of course, I didn't know what the problem was, but I knew I was a part of 'we' and was about to be enlightened.

"We" have a 600-pound steer in the northeast corner of the farm with pneumonia. "We" need to get him closer to the house, aka the corral. Without hesitation, I grabbed some jeans and rubber boots and hustled out the door. I was then informed that the rancher had no plan for how we were going to handle this task. The steer was too fast to catch, too big to rope, and, well, we couldn't just tell him, "Go to the house!" like we do the dog. That's when I wanted to say, "When you figure it out, let me know... I've got things to do," but the divine duct tape was firmly in place. So, when he paused, I suggested we assess the situation and come up with a plan. I'm all about plans, whether it's A, B, or even D—sometimes.

We arrived at the paddock where the cattle were happily grazing and quickly spotted the big boy and his momma, immediately acting on no plan, opening gates and herding them toward the corral. I might add that when cattle are intensively grazed, getting them to move to a previous paddock is nearly impossible. It's kind of like eating a good salad one day, then being handed the leftovers the next day and expecting enthusiastic eating. The unplanned plan was working. Open a gate, momma and baby walk through. Three paddocks later, their 'enthusiasm' was waning, and they started to balk. If you've ever tried to run in rubber boots through a recently grazed pasture, you know things can get a little slippery. For some reason, sliding down a hill on recycled 'grass and water' causes every muscle, except the bladder, to tighten. Momma and baby were scared to come any closer to me and my screeching and headed to the next paddock. It was at this point that I wished I had my new 'sign-on bonus' gift from my boss. I'm not exactly sure what it's called, but I refer to it as my cattle paddle.

It looks good on the porch but is not very effective there. So, the journey continues as I walk with my two blue electric fence posts and my arms outstretched, trying to be large and in charge while the boss follows along on the four-wheeler.

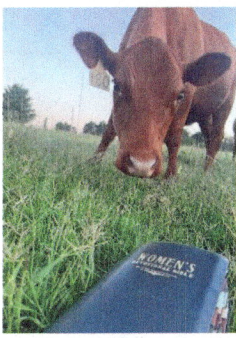

The divine duct tape is wearing thin as I am instructed to not rush the steer because he has pneumonia, and we don't want him to breathe heavily. All I can think about is that I need to leave town shortly, and I am not even packed, showered, or remotely ready. It doesn't seem to be a problem that I am breathing heavily. I began to pray for all those things that I am supposed to be at this moment, with the exception of 'on time'. I guess you could say I prayer-walked our farm, along with a little cardio and resistance training. I began to think I was using my time for a little more than just ranch work. Once in the corral, my man gave me the go-ahead to take the day off, and he'd finish up. I had to laugh as he sighed, "That went way better than I ever thought it would." I walked off the job with the following resignation: "I serve a God that not only can move mountains, He can move cows too." I rushed inside to get all those things, well, the most important things done and was on my way.

I'm happy to report that the big boy is better and I had an amazing weekend. And yes, duct tape does fix everything!

I am just so in awe of Him every day!

MY JOURNAL

What made me laugh today

_____

_____

_____

What am I grateful for

_____

_____

_____

_____

_____

Smells like Money

At Wormington Farms, calving begins in early spring, meaning there is always a chance of late snow to make conditions anything but desirable for a newborn calf. Momma cows are rather smart when it comes to birthing babies, but their idea of a maternity ward is not necessarily the most hygienic of conditions, like the mud pit that surrounds a hay feeder. This particular season, there were several newborns that required the neonatal intensive care unit, otherwise known as my basement. I'm not a nurse, just the farm wife, and my job was to dry these fragile little wet babies with clean towels and feed them warm colostrum in a bottle or tube in hopes that they would fight for their life.

We had routine maternity checks, but it seemed the 10:00 PM check had the most action. I remember one particular evening, the weather was wet and cold, and my man offered to make rounds. I had just crawled into my cozy, warm bed when I heard the all-too-familiar sound of my name being yelled in a tone that meant STAT! I knew exactly what that meant: the farmer was holding a wet, nearly lifeless calf, standing at the door, hoping for a miracle. I jumped out of bed, rushed to the door to the laundry room, only to discover that someone had left the dryer door open. At that point, we were both yelling. I hobbled to the door, and we managed to get the little one to the basement and start the process I had become all too familiar with. I mentioned the continual massage of the calf to not only dry it off but to increase circulation and the tube of warm colostrum, but I didn't mention the motivational speech? The speech was only intended for the little calf that I held as I looked into its big brown eyes and incredibly long eyelashes, but to my surprise, it was heard throughout the house by anyone standing close to one of the heater vents upstairs in the kitchen.

Once the snow melts and the grass turns green, the calves start to frolic, and I know spring is just around the corner. Spring of 2003 brought lots of calves with unique markings, thanks to our Beef master bull, Hutch (purchased from our friend, Mark Hutchings). Several had brown or white patches around their eyes and white tips on their tails. Speaking of tails, when checking for healthy calves, it was important that those white tips remained white because too much of a green grass thing can make those tails a different color. Bottom line meaning: Scours. This particular season, the farmer was getting quite frustrated with the mini epidemic. It seemed these fast little bovines were sick but not slow. Catching them was a challenge. One evening, he asked his little princess to help him. It wasn't long before I heard a banging on the kitchen door. I quickly opened it to see her standing on the porch, huffing and puffing as if she had run to the house. Between breaths, she quickly told me of the events that had just happened while holding up her dad's wallet between two fingers. The wallet was covered in... well, let's just say it didn't smell like money, although some farmers may disagree. The story goes that dad caught a calf, the calf's hoof caught his back pocket and ripped his pants, and the wallet went flying and landed in a pile of #3. She exclaimed as she flew out of sight, "And DAD is MAD!" I took the wallet and proceeded to salvage what I could. And for those who are not mathematical wizards, #3 is a combination of #1 + #2. On the farm, we call that Scours. It wasn't until the farmer walked through the door that I got the full picture. The back of his pants was missing, and the white flag of surrender was showing. The bottom line now... his little girl saw him lose his temper, something we don't see very often on the farm, and that cost more than the pair of 'good' jeans that had been destroyed.

The wife in me wanted to remind him that he should never wear good jeans to check calves, but the love in me admired the man who saw a relationship more important than a possession.

Spring is coming, and with it comes new life, for which we are thankful.

MY JOURNAL

What made me laugh today

_____

_____

_____

What am I grateful for

_____

_____

_____

_____

_____

_____

Stirring the Pot

I never really knew what that meant until my glamorous life went down the toilet.

The love of my life and I escaped for a weekend in the wilderness. Actually, we took our RV to Roaring River State Park. I know it is only 30 minutes away from home, but deep in the woods with no cell phone, television, or radio reception, it felt like we were far away. That meant no fence building, no cattle to move, no laundry, and no housework—total relaxation. Just what every farmer and his wife long for. Friday, we arrived in time to grill some supper and take a walk. Saturday, we woke up to a great outdoor breakfast and did a little hiking.

The Captain and his first mate took a three-hour tour from Eagle Rock to Table Rock Lake in the canoe. There were no Ginger or Marianne, just Taco the dog, who wasn't thrilled about the canoe ride but even less thrilled about the water. We waded through the swampy mud, carrying our canoe until we were able to make the big launch. If I listened closely, I could hear the Deliverance music playing in the background.

I was convinced that I was just along for the ride and would be the figurehead of this ship, but once again, I was wrong. Yes, I said it: "I was wrong," and now it's in writing, but that's another story for another time. I should have known that with one set of paddles and one fishing rod, someone was going to have to work. I began to paddle as the "captain" fished. With every cast, the canoe would move from side to side, and then the dog would move from front to back. I was pretty certain that a giant carp would eat us if we capsized in this stagnant, swampy water. I felt much more confident as we entered the lake water until we were greeted by a boat with a motor, resulting in large waves. Large is all in the eyes of the beholder, and I was the one about to behold the paddle in the little canoe.

We managed to travel quite a distance, then decided to take a purposeful dip to cool off in the refreshing lake water. Once back in the canoe, we headed for camp. After a great dinner on the grill and a shower, we decided to call it a night. Just as I lay my head on the pillow, I hear the pitter-patter of itty bitty feet. I peeked out the window to see three little raccoons trying on my man's shoes for size. The little Cinderellas had no luck and went on their way.

Sunday morning, I awoke to my man's cooking again. I am starting to like this camping concept. We thought we would attempt to trout fish. An attempt is exactly what we did. I think I prefer lake fishing, as you can't see what you are about to not catch. After a nap, we decided to head back to civilization and reality, but not before first stopping at the dump station. Ahhh, the luxuries of camping in an RV are sometimes short-lived. Makes one rethink tent camping, pit toilets, and trees. Usually, this is not a big deal, but for some reason, stuff wasn't flowing as usual. That is when a woman's work is never done! The captain gave me a long stick and told me I was going to have to stir the pot. You've heard the saying, "$#$%^$ flows downhill," and it did, finally!

Once again, all is well that ends well. We had a great weekend together and a greater appreciation for the finer things in life, like indoor plumbing.

MY JOURNAL

What made me laugh today
_____
_____
_____

What am I grateful for
_____
_____
_____
_____
_____
_____

Birthin' Babies

According to the famous quote in Gone with the Wind, "I don't know nothin' 'bout birthin' no babies." I do know this: at Wormington Farms, the cows and heifers seem to know when it is most inconvenient to birth their babies. After dark, in wet, wintry weather, when I have a 'to-do' list longer than the day is long, or when I have plans to go somewhere. It appears it is all about me—obviously NOT!

Prime example: The boss and I were going to go to the bull rides with the kids and dinner with the parents. After showering and making myself presentable, the farmer comes through the door and announces, "The party is over." I didn't think it had even started. We have a cow trying to calve, and things don't look normal. I was anything but enthusiastic about this event with the comment from my man, "Think of it this way, your hair will look good while you're pulling a calf." We called off the plans, and instead of putting on my best jeans, I put on the old jeans, rubber boots, jacket, and gloves and headed outside. Did I mention it was snowing? Teamwork was on our side as we got the cow in the corral and assessed the situation. Assessing was difficult as the calf was not only backwards but upside down inside the birth canal. Things were getting messy, and my tiny bit of enthusiasm was diminishing as my hands and feet started getting cold. My job is very important: I am the designated tail holder. The pay stinks, but nevertheless, it is an important job, and the security, well, I know as long as there is a tail and it is covered in grass and water, I'll be holding it. You do know what grass plus water equals when it comes to a cow's tail? Let's just say, it's not the smell of a spring day. My friend Donna shared this equation with me. She is the one who "wanted" to marry a farmer. I'll call it like it is, the tail is covered in #$%#% and it stinks, and I have to hold it. When I am not holding it, things can get real messy quickly. When the tail starts flying, those involved in labor and delivery start ducking. If you have never had a feeling like something wet just landed on your cheek, you've never experienced life on the farm at its most glamorous. I knew WE had made the right choice to cancel our plans, but there was no consolation as we pulled the calf, and it wasn't alive. That always makes for a sad day on the farm.

We've had many successful births since then. I love watching the newborn calves run and play. It is especially funny when they manage to escape their momma's under the electric fence and they soon get a scolding. To you and me, it sounds like a long moo, but I'm sure in cow language it resembles, 'I told you to lie down right here and stay, don't move until I tell you to'.

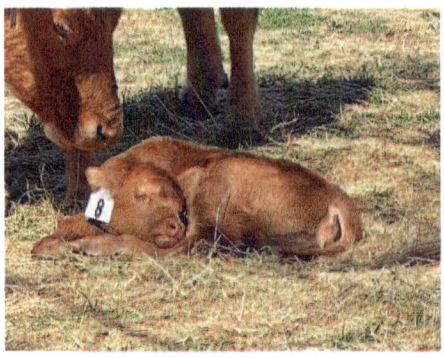

Saturday, I was reminded that I am enslaved to the cows. I had done the usual housework and was about to shower and get ready to run some errands when I noticed from the kitchen window a heifer acting a little strange. Calving heifers always get extra attention on our farm. Fortunately, I could watch her from the comfort of my kitchen. So, I kept an eye on her in between showering and eating some lunch. Sure enough, just minutes before I was to head out the door, she went into labor. I continued to watch her, and her progression was not as speedy as I would have liked. I prayed for a successful delivery, knowing that was the only option since I was home alone. I continued to watch out the window and through the binoculars as the water bag broke and the front feet and head emerged. At that point, I started yelling for the momma to push. I doubt she could hear me, but I felt like I was doing something proactive. It seemed forever before the process was completed. Upon the sigh of relief after delivery, I noticed the momma had not gotten up, and the calf needed to be licked and loved. So, I headed out to check on the calf. Halfway between the house and the calf, in the rain, I noticed the new momma getting up and starting to lick her baby. I returned to the house to watch patiently. Patience soon ran out as I noticed she was licking the wrong end. She needed to start at the head to make sure the placenta was away from the nose so the calf could breathe. In my frustration, I wanted to yell, "Don't make me have to come back out there and show you how it is done." The new momma had enough God-given instincts to know what to do, and she persisted until she got the job done. She licked her new baby for hours until they both finally tired and lay down next to each other. By this time, I had missed my appointment, but there would be another day. Sure enough, the following Saturday, the same scenario.

The little critters are enjoying the spring-like weather. The farmer found one hiding between two round bales of hay. He thought he would cut it off in its path and make it go back under the fence to its momma. To his surprise, the two-day-old calf bellered and butted him in the shins. A whole new meaning to 'the terrible twos'.

I must tell you, the cows run this farm, and it is pretty evident this time of year that they are in control of the time clock. We don't venture far from home for very long. Spring is just around the corner, and for that, we are thankful. We love experiencing the new births on the farm, flowers, and greener pastures.

MY JOURNAL

What made me laugh today

_____
_____
_____

What am I grateful for

_____
_____
_____
_____
_____
_____

The Mechanic

He can pull an engine, but can he pull a calf?

If Murphy's law is "If anything can go wrong, it will," then the farmer's wife's law should be "When the farmer is away, the cows WILL get out or go into labor."

It was a nice spring day, and my man and our daughters were gone. I had the day all to myself! I had a list of things to accomplish, one of which was sleeping late. I got up at 4 a.m. to see him off as he headed to a farm equipment sale in Illinois. I took a little nap once he left the driveway. I did morning chores and enjoyed breakfast in my new rocking chair on the front porch. Things were going just as planned until I noticed a heifer looked as if she was contemplating calving. The closer I looked, I could tell this wasn't going to happen anytime soon. In the meantime, I went to check the cows and noticed one of them was contemplating the same. No need to take a shower, as the events to come could be messy. "Waiting" was not on my agenda.

In order to overcome my impatience, I grabbed a bag of pork rinds and a Diet Coke and planted myself on the swing set in the backyard to watch the progress of the heifer, who was in the pasture directly behind the house, and pray that God would intervene so I wouldn't have to. The dogs sat around waiting for a treat, and Jack the donkey stuck his head through the fence, waiting for a handout or a pet. It was then that I saw some progress with the heifer and decided to go for a closer look. I could tell the calf was breech, and the heifer was no longer attempting to push. I tried to get her into the birthing room, aka The Barn, but my four-legged helper, Scooby the dog, hindered the effort. I referred to my calving notes taped to the refrigerator and knew time was critical. I called the farmer in a panic, but he was still too far from home to be of help. I knew how he desired to have a 100% calf crop, and we were so close. I could not find any assistance and, giving in, called the vet. In the meantime, my farmer husband called his friend Ken, the mechanic, a novice farmer like myself. At this point, I found no comfort, only an increased level of stress. God was not going to answer my prayer, and a mechanic was coming to my rescue? All I could think of was, sure, he can pull an engine, but can he pull a calf? I got everything ready, and we were able to get the young mama-to-be in the barn. She was not happy with the situation and hit the metal gate, which, in turn, hit both of us. Had I not been hanging on to the head squeeze for dear life, we would have both been knocked down in the mud. We managed to put the squeeze on her, and with all my commands, or shall I say instructions, Ken was able to successfully pull the calf. When mama and baby began to bond, we left the two alone.

Once outside the barn, I turned to thank Ken, only to hear him release a big sigh and deliver the statement, "I have got to have a cigarette!" I found that most hilarious. I called the vet to cancel the farm call and continued to thank our mechanic friend and reassure him that I couldn't have done it by myself, despite my "know-it-all" commands or bossiness during delivery. His kind response was that he was happy to help, and by the way, he had never pulled a calf before. There is something to be said about a woman's intuition!

After he left, I began to pick up things, and it was then I remembered the cow that was contemplating calving earlier. I walked down into the field where she was, and sure enough, feet were out, and they were in the right position. I came in the house to rest a bit and call my dad, who loves to remind me that I once said, "I would never marry a farmer." Later in the day, I went back outside to check the cattle. The cow and her new calf were fine. The new baby in the barn needed to be tube-fed; it was too weak to get up and suck from his mama. I called my father-in-law, who is always more likely to help if bribery with a pie is involved. I went out to the pasture one more time before dark, and all was well in the maternity ward. The new mama had her baby snuggled in the hay, anticipating cooler weather. The last cow/calf check will be waiting for the one who loves to farm when he returns home later tonight. Grateful for good friends and family who come to my rescue on the ranch.

MY JOURNAL

What made me laugh today

_____
_____
_____

What am I grateful for

_____
_____
_____
_____
_____
_____

2 Daughters 2 Weddings 2 Weeks

Two daughters, two weddings, two weeks – it's too much! This was the time I knew I had raised my girls to be independent and resourceful, and for that, I was thankful.

I have to give you a little background on the girls, as their personalities played a big role in creating a very special day. Daughter #2 was the first to get married; she had been planning for several months, and the details were perfectly Pinterest-worthy. As she stated, "If you want it done right, you have to do it yourself." And she did, for the most part. Daughter #1 was the second to get married, and she had yet to begin—she's a bit of a procrastinator. I might add that she planned her wedding within a week. And yes, she was running late on her wedding day, which was no surprise to anyone.

Daughter #2 had a theme of black, white, red, and bling, a wedding with all the trimmings. Daughter #1 had a country-themed wedding and was married in a barn with everything simple.

Both daughters were beautiful, and we delighted in their happiness. Dad, on the other hand, well, once he's out from under the sedation, I'll let you know. Actually, he did quite well, from giving his blessings to the boys who asked for it to walking his daughters down the aisles. Fortunately, the lump in his throat wasn't so big that he couldn't say who gave the bride. He even managed a daddy-daughter dance. I might add, this is the man who learned how to dance from Bill Cosby.

I had to laugh when telling my dentist about two daughters, two weddings in two weeks. His response was, "What were you thinking?" Oddly enough, no one asked what I was thinking.

Many ask how we afforded such celebrations so close together. Keep in mind that both girls chose spring weddings, the busiest time of the year for the milkman and farmer/rancher. He gave both daughters a specific head of cattle and told them to make sure he knows when and where to show up on the big day. They could choose to sell the cattle and spend the money on a wedding, house, or investment. They could also choose to start their own herd. I'll let you figure out who did what.

From these events, I took away some funny and fabulous memories. I was asked not to take up the whole page in the guestbook that asks for the parents of the bride to give their advice. Remember, there are four parents who have to write on this one little page. I cherished that 'our' wedding song was played again. And when push comes to shove, I learned a new phrase: "Put it in Pam mode." I took that as a compliment from my daughters—that when something needs to get done, that's the mode we should all be in. Apparently, they have become familiar with it over the years.

In the midst of the wedding planning and preparation, I got to step back and watch two grown girls play out their dreams, make decisions on their own, have a tantrum or two, and at the end of the day, they were married to the men they love and desire to spend the rest of their life with here on earth. The men whom we have prayed for over the years, long before we even knew their names, the men we trust to be the spiritual leaders of their home, and the men who will protect and provide for our daughters.

A few years later, we are blessed that these two daughters have shared with us three grandsons.

MY JOURNAL

What made me laugh today

_____

_____

_____

_____

What am I grateful for

_____

_____

_____

_____

_____

_____

Birthin' Babies Part 2

It was another spring day, and the farmer just happened to be out of town. I performed the routine morning cow/calf check and the other chores as assigned. I was ready to enjoy the rest of my day alone, doing a few things on my 'to-do' list, when the boss called and said the meetings were over and he would be coming home soon. I mentioned that I thought a couple of cows would calve by the time he arrived.

Women's intuition told me to make one more check before taking a shower. I noticed a cow calving in the field and watched from the truck while giving the farmer a play-by-play on the cell phone. "All is well," I reported while the other cow was in labor, and everything seemed fine. I headed for the house, excited about the long-awaited shower and ME time.

After showering, I peeked out the kitchen window and noticed the old cow's water sack was out, but there was no progress, so I thought I'd better analyze the situation a little closer. Two feet were out, and they were facing upward. I knew this meant the calf was breech and I would need help. The farmer was an hour away, the brother-in-law was 30 minutes away, and you guessed it, the mechanic was available. I got everything ready for the delivery. The round-up was an adventure. Over the hills and through the fences, but not in the corral, was this old girl going. At the point of giving up, the mechanic and I noticed the farmer and his friend arriving, pulling into the driveway. This friend had just mentioned that he would like to see a calf born. I say, "Be careful what you wish for!" The brother-in-law arrived soon, and the rodeo score was now 1 to 5. The 1 was winning, and the 5 were exhausted as they chased and attempted to corral the birthing mother. We were certain the calf was probably not alive due to the time lapse in the birth canal and the stress of the cow. That is when frustration sets in, and the determination to save the cow gives the farmer and his wife the energy to press on.

The brother-in-law had a brilliant idea to lasso the cow. Funny, I thought you had to have a horse to pull off that stunt, and all we had was a miniature mule. That is not a vision one wants to have when all is serious. Miniature was the route we took, not the mule, but the Mitsubishi mini truck. The farmer was driving the truck as his brother knelt in the back, swirling the rope over his head. Over the hills and through the field they went, and around the cow's neck the rope landed. The runaway cow was still winning as the farmer jumped out of the truck and grabbed the end of the rope from his brother. You may not be able to roller skate in a buffalo herd, as the old song says, but you can ski on fresh green grass. The cow pulled the farmer at a rate of speed that was incomprehensible through the field until the big hedge tree presented itself. My resourceful man and his quick-thinking

mind wrapped the rope around the tree, and the four men pulled on the rope until they laid the laboring cow down. Now the score was Cowboys 5 and Cow 1. I quickly ran to get the calving chains, but all the manpower could not extract the breeched calf. I ran again to get the pullers, and at that point, success was achieved. To our surprise, the baby was alive. Two men held the calf up by the hind legs as my man cleared the airway. No, he didn't do mouth-to-mouth. After much yelling and screaming in delight, we caught our breath and released the momma to be with her new baby. Unfortunately, she had nothing to do with any of us or the calf. She walked in the opposite direction. At that point, my job had just begun. I tried to dry off the baby and get its circulation flowing. I then headed to the house to warm up some stored colostrum.

The baby and I met in the barn, and I continued to warm it, rub it, and feed it. It had a lot of determination to live, and I had a lot of determination to do all I could to make it happen. Momma cow later joined us and decided to bond with her baby. My job was done; all is well that ends well. Tomorrow, I am taking a Comp Day, without pay, of course.

MY JOURNAL

What made me laugh today

_____

_____

_____

What am I grateful for

_____

_____

_____

_____

_____

_____

The Cows are out!

Do the words "cows are out" make your hair stand on end? One night, my "I forgot to shut the gate" husband came running into the house, yelling, "Cows are out." We grabbed run-down flashlights that barely emitted light, in my estimation, less than a candle, and ran outside into the darkness. My brave husband jumped on the four-wheeler and left my daughter and me walking in the dark, looking for the black cows. Just before he made his quick escape to the opposite end of the pasture, he informed us that he would herd the cattle toward us and we were to get them into the designated field, but be sure not to shine the flashlight in their eyes. "But wait, how are they going to see me?" There is nothing comforting about a herd of black cattle running toward you in the dark. If I can't shine the flashlight in their eyes, where am I supposed to shine it? During this episode, I had taken comfort in the fact that I was not alone in the situation. My daughter was right beside me, right? Wrong. Once the task was complete, I discovered she had taken refuge in the back of the pickup. I should have been shining my flashlight on her.

Photo Credit to Alan Ader

Not too long after this, I was getting ready to go somewhere and had just gotten out of the shower when I heard the all-too-familiar sound of my husband yelling, "Cows are out." It was raining, so I grabbed some clothes and a raincoat, left the towel on my just-washed hair, and ran out the door. At the same time, our neighbor had noticed the cattle running by his front door, so he came out to help. All I could think about was the old saying, "First impressions are lasting impressions." What an impression I must be making. Once we succeeded in herding the cattle back through the open gate, I informed my husband that if he can't remember to shut the gate, he doesn't need to be raising cattle. I'm sure that statement made no impression.

One cold winter morning, early, we leapt out of bed as we heard such a clatter that you would think Santa was on the roof. If only! Rather, it was a passerby banging on the door, yelling, what else but "Cows are out!" We grabbed our boots and coats and headed out for the roundup, the same black cows. As I was running around, I felt this funny bobbing on top of my head and remembered I had gone to bed with wet hair, and the bobbing feeling was a result of how my hair had dried. Did I mention it was winter and cold? I was sure glad it was dark and the neighbor was nowhere around. As we finished the roundup, my husband discovered that the gate must have been left open. Amazing how he recognizes the obvious just a little too late. I suddenly remembered, Taco, the dog, barking continuously during the night. So much so that we made him come in the house so we could get some sleep. If only that dog could speak, I'm sure he would say, "I tried to tell you the cows are out."

MY JOURNAL

What made me laugh today
_____
_____
_____
_____

What am I grateful for
_____
_____
_____
_____
_____
_____
_____

A Hanging at Wormington Farms

How many times have I heard, "Can you just ride in the tractor with me and open the gates?" "Come help me, it will only take a minute." "No need to change clothes, I just need you to help tag a calf." The answer would be too many times to not know better. It will take more than a minute, you should change into work clothes, and who wants to be the gate boss? And how much intelligence does that take, because how much skill does that really require? Apparently, more than I have.

It was a cold, wintry day, and the boss beckoned me to JUST watch the gate while he fed hay so that there would be no escaping cattle. So, I bundled up, and we jumped in the old 2-105 White tractor and headed up the hill. We got to the gate, and I opened the tractor door and proceeded to jump out, but to my surprise, the hood of my Carhart was caught on the door latch. Yes, I was dangling from the tractor door. My feet barely reached the ground, and the zipper to my coat was wrapped around my neck. My sympathetic husband simply reached over, unhooked me, and let me drop to the ground upon my loud request.

As I made my way to the gate, I looked back toward the tractor to see him doubled over in the cab. No, he was not having a heart attack; he was laughing hysterically. As usual, I was not laughing. I was a 38-year-old married woman with a hickey mark that resembled a zipper around my neck.

This was not the only incident at this gate that required some intelligence and skill. On another occasion, I was summoned to gate duty. As with most rotational grazing systems, we use a lot of electric fence and some gates, mainly a high-tensile wire that is smooth. But this particular gate was an old galvanized gate that swung open next to a stretch of barbed wire. Not thinking for a moment that the barbed wire could be electric, I proceeded to hook the gate to it. It didn't take this city girl long to figure out things aren't always as they seem, and what felt like a flash of lightning coursing through my body caused me to say words foreign to my everyday vocabulary. Once again, I looked up in the tractor to see the boss doubled over, crying on my behalf. No, they were not tears of sympathy.

My question of the day would be: Why is it so funny when someone else gets shocked by an electric fence? Think about it. The boss has a new t-shirt that he so deservingly wears, and it reads… "It's funny until someone gets hurt, and then it is hilarious." I might mention there is no workman's comp on this farm. The only compensation I ever see is a hug, a kiss, and a giggly apology for laughing at my mistakes.

MY JOURNAL

What made me laugh today
_____
_____
_____

What am I grateful for
_____
_____
_____
_____
_____
_____

It's Not Over Until The Yelling Stops

A few years ago, my husband informed me that he isn't a Farmer, he is a Rancher. He clarified for me that a Farmer works the land and typically produces a crop; he, on the other hand, works with cattle. Well, thank you for letting me walk beside you for 20-some years before enlightening me. Now, what am I supposed to do with those personalized license plates, FRMWIF?

Call it what you may, but I'm going to tell you that working cattle together involves tasks and words that I never thought I would experience as a wife. Let me just clarify one thing: I will try every excuse under the sun to get out of this chore, and here are a few reasons why. It is not natural to stand in front of a herd of animals, each weighing in about four times as much as you, that have twice as many legs and can run a lot faster. I don't care how big your stick is! And while we're at it, who designed those little skinny sticks for working cattle? How effective is that going to be against a mad momma or a big bull? I really like the paddle on a stick my man got me as a sign-on bonus when I quit my real job to work on the RANCH with him. It's plastic and has noisy little beads in the paddle portion attached to the long plastic stick. I can assure you, seeing a fly swatter come toward your backside is far scarier than that, and it doesn't take a very big bovine to bend that thing. Just call me Consumer Reports because I tested it and I know.

Photo Credit To Alan Ader

Enough about the equipment, let's talk about the working conditions. Sunny and warm temps are not the norm, because we wouldn't want to overheat the cattle or the cowgirls. With those weather conditions also come pesky flies, because I know where the flies have landed and where they are likely to land. I don't care if the first location is covered in a combination of grass and water; I don't want the second location to be on my lips. However, it is likely it will be on my glasses. I originally thought the squeeze chute was designed to hold the cattle while you 'worked' on them. It turns out, it was designed to squeeze out the water and grass concoction from the cows that will eventually be shared by a swishing tail, flies, or rubber boots that weren't made for walking through this slick stuff. Those boots need some brakes!

If you are a wife and you live with a cattle rancher/farmer, unless you are as smart as my mother-in-law and sister-in-law, who declined the assignment up front in their marriage vows, then you know what the conversation can be like in the corral. I try to convince myself that the volume must be loud to be heard over the bellering bovine. But the more I think about it, there are a lot of things that I really don't need to hear. For example, I don't want to hear the nicknames for the cows that don't understand where or what they are supposed to do. These are not terms of endearment. Furthermore, calling the cattle names just uses up excess energy that I don't have. I also don't need to hear the critiquing of my capabilities and how I should run faster, be more aggressive, stop a stampede, or make a rusty head squeeze operate smoothly and swiftly.

I could go on and on, and I still wouldn't get fired from this 'farming' job. At the end of the day, when each head of cattle has been tended to and is turned out on fresh grass and water, it's a good feeling. A shower and a warm, soft bed always help my attitude. I'm thankful my raging rancher always apologizes for any slip-ups while working cattle and is always amazed at my city girl suggestions, when they work.

MY JOURNAL

What made me laugh today

_____

_____

_____

What am I grateful for

_____

_____

_____

_____

_____

Pausing for a Plan

Was a nice fall day, perfect for camping at The Pines with our friends. That's exactly what we were doing until I heard, "Let's make hay while the sun shines." We paused our glamping and drove home to Missouri to do just that, one of those quick jobs that "won't take very long." Only 16 acres, 4 tractors, 2 balers, 2 people, plus the neighbor and his dog, and a sunny day. We used up all the daylight but got the job done, though not without some excitement and complaining.

My frugal farmer got a 'new-to-him' side delivery rake that would supposedly save us time. My math skills were far from par when he started explaining how four rows of hay become one, with row one going on top of row two, and row four going on top of row three. Then you take the V rake and make all four rows become one. If the math wasn't enough to make my head hurt, driving different tractors and watching the half rake behind me was enough to give me a stiff neck.

A few rounds and a pattern started to develop, and that's when he decided to switch things up a bit. I jumped on a different tractor to try out the 'new-to-him' square baler.  Things were going smoothly, so we switched things up again and tried out the 'new-to-him' round baler with the old rake and the old tractor, ahhhh, something that I was somewhat familiar with. The raking part went well, but the baling part, not so much. Let's just say once that neatly raked hay is pulled out of the guts of the round baler, it must be raked again in order to make a new hay bale. No math needed to figure out the time involved with raking, baling, unbaling, raking the same hay again, and baling it a second time. It only took one round of the field to discover this wasn't going to work. Time, fuel, sweat, and frustration all come at a cost.

Our neighbor, George, and his dog Jack just stopped by to get in on the excitement. I've discovered farming is always better from the other side of the fence, watching someone else and their wife work cattle, make hay, or whatever the task is that tries an otherwise happy marriage.

In the meantime, I was in the side-by-side, which is equipped with a winch that makes cleaning out a clogged baler a bit easier. While the winch was doing its thing, I noticed George had come prepared with snacks. Yep, I was eyeing his apple that looked like something from Snow White, but what I was really coveting was the chocolate bar that was lying on the dash. I was getting hungry and could use some cheese with my whine, and by this time in the day, I had a lot of whine. We didn't bring snacks for this 'it won't take long' job. But George didn't offer, and I didn't partake.

Back to Plan A, or B+, not quite sure, but I square baled the remainder of the field, and the young 60-something guys hopped on and off the wagon and loaded the square bales, laughing and thinking about how much they were going to feel the effects of physical labor much more than they did in their younger hay-hauling days.

The best part of the day was when George told me that his Uncle JW would be proud of me baling hay. You see, in my younger married days, I would rake hay, and JW would drive behind me, baling whatever mess I raked. My precision farmer just shook his head, commenting that if I raked tic-tac-toe in the field, JW would follow me and bale, laughing all the time until he was paid with homemade cookies at the end of the day. I sure miss JW, his patience, and his laughter.

Farm life isn't always easy or convenient, but friends make the load lighter.

MY JOURNAL

What made me laugh today
_____
_____
_____

What am I grateful for
_____
_____
_____
_____
_____
_____

Baby in the Beans

It was a hot summer day, and as usual, I had it all planned... we were to go camping as soon as the farmer finished hauling milk. And since I was off work that day, I knew I would have it all in order when the time came to leave: groceries bought, camper packed, chores complete. That's how every good, organized, and in-control farmer's wife would do it.

Then I got a call from the farmer saying that his dad had lost a calf in the bean field, and due to the high temps, he'd really like it if I could go assist him. How could I resist? I owed it to my father-in-law, as many times as he had come to my rescue. Besides, I was already dressed for the occasion, workout clothes and Boggs. I'm pretty sure the hot pink in my shorts matched the floral print in my boots. Fashion on the farm is key.

After combing the bean field, sweating, and seeing mirages of calves blowing in the wind, a friendly passerby slowed to ask us if 'that' was our calf lying in the ditch. With a quick response, "YES," we changed our course, forgetting to ask where it was lying. I walked up and down the road to no avail. I then had that sick feeling that someone was playing a terrible joke on us. I got the jeep and drove up and down the road a few times, watching my father-in-law do the same on the four-wheeler, as well as my mother-in-law on foot. Then, all of a sudden, my eyes were drawn to the calf lying in the ditch where it last lost contact with my father-in-law hours ago. I jumped out of the jeep and thought to myself, as I approached the motionless calf, that it must be dead. To my surprise, as I reached down to touch it, it leapt to life and began running down the road. Thankfully, a neighbor was coming from the other direction, and she was familiar with the farm scene. She stopped her vehicle and jumped out as we tried to head the calf to the field where it belonged. Naturally, that was not the direction it wanted to go. As it leaped to the fence of the bean field, she grabbed it by the back legs, and I ran to assist. With lots of bawling, my father-in-law noticed the commotion and came to our rescue. We hog-tied the little calf, which was so heavy it took all three of us to lift it onto the four-wheeler. To keep the little one still and in place, the original farmer sat on it and drove it back to the field where its momma resided. Nothing like a little rodeo on a hot summer day to get the blood pumping.

At that point, I returned home to plan B. I wasn't sure what that was, but I knew I didn't have enough time for plan A anymore. I had a good feeling that I had returned one of many favors and was glad to help. I later heard that the momma would no longer accept her baby after several tries that afternoon on the part of my father-in-law. I felt bad for him as he tried so hard to save the little calf and bring it back to its momma for nutrition and nurturing. I was then reminded why ranchers keep log books with all their cattle records. But who looks at the book when we think we know everything? Unfortunately, we were matching the corralled calf with the wrong momma. Two wrongs don't make a right, no matter how you do the math.

At the end of the day, all is well and everyone is where they need to be: cows, calves, and ranchers camping around a campfire.

MY JOURNAL

What made me laugh today
_____
_____
_____

What am I grateful for
_____
_____
_____
_____
_____
_____

Deep Doo Doo

As you know, we haven't had a shortage of rain this Spring in the Ozarks. On a cattle farm, mix that with the remnants of a herd of cows, and you get an abundance of muck. I have probably mentioned that we intensively graze our cattle. What that means is we have small areas of our farm fenced off, and we allow cows to graze on a paddock of fresh greens daily, sometimes twice daily. Joel Salatin refers to it as Salad Bar beef. It also allows our cows to maintain a girlish figure. They are just like humans; they like routine, and when they hear us in the field, they expect us to open a gate and allow them to start grazing on fresh green pasture.

The rancher asked me to move the cows a couple of days ago while he was gone hauling milk. Thinking about the environment, I chose to take the mini truck to do the job. My logical thinking was that it has four-wheel drive, I would be enclosed should the muck start flying, and whatever supplies I would need, they would be in the bed of the little pickup, along with many other supplies totally unnecessary. I also remember him saying, while giving the instructions, that I would need to tie the gate to the fence, as the cows would probably not be eager to move to my chosen paddock. So, this girl and her dog got in the truck and headed out to the field. I arrived at the destination to hear the loud greetings of a herd of hungry cows. I got out of the truck, waded through the muck with my ratchet straps, and opened the gate. It was a stampede!!! I flung the straps around the gate, pulled them tight, and stood in the gap so that the cows would head on into the appropriate paddock. Feeling quite confident that I had managed to move the cows just like I was asked. Well, with the exception of the baby calves that run and play hide-n-seek with the mommas and catch me if you can under the electric fence.

I got in the truck to head back to the house, only to discover that I'm stuck in the muck. No problem, I'll just put it in four-wheel drive. That's when I discovered the lever didn't work. So I started searching for something to put in front of the tires to make traction. After that didn't work, I thought to myself, it is a mini truck, I'll get out and push, and that didn't work either. When all else fails, call the boss. I believe his loud response was, "Of all the choices, why did you take the mini truck?" I could tell he really didn't want to know my response, so I just hung up the phone. It was at that point that I abandoned ship. Me and my dog walked or waded back to the house, with little curious calves following us. This is when I realized I was in deep doo-doo, literally!

Just like a kid who waits for the other parent to get home to dish out their punishment, I waited for the rancher to get home so WE could get the truck unstuck. Just as time or luck would have it, we ate supper, and then I had to run to Bible study. Thank the Lord! The boss walked to the truck in the field while I was gone, thinking he would rescue it, but unfortunately had to walk back to the house empty-handed.

The next morning rolls around, and we head out to the field with the old faithful jeep and a chain. Oh wait, did I mention that when I left the truck, I also left the key on? Yep, now we have a dead battery, too.

Chain to the front, pull, pull, pull, and no success. Chain to the back, pull, pull, pull, and no success. "You drive the jeep, and I will drive the truck; you drive the truck, and I'll drive the jeep." After several attempts at what appeared to be a Chinese fire drill, the jeep pulls the mini truck out of the muck into a field with a little less mess. Remember, the battery is dead, so now we have to get the tractor to pull the truck uphill and back to the barn. Let's just say, I didn't need a workout this morning because my adrenal glands were working overtime. As I steered the truck, I looked directly at the spears on the back of the tractor in front of me, thinking, if something goes less than ideal, I could be another farm casualty. And we know I already asked to be the fired hired hand, and that didn't work. The tractor driver kept glancing back at me with a slight grin. I wasn't sure whether to smile or cry.

Thinking back on my choice, to prevent making the same mistake twice, I asked, "So how can you tell if the truck is in four-wheel drive if the lever doesn't work?" His response was, "The nail is on the dash." Let's just say that would have never crossed my mind. Ranchers are resourceful, and apparently, you can engage and disengage your drive with a simple nail.

Back at the barn, the little truck safely tucked away, we considered the task finished. I apologize again, and my rancher husband gives me a kiss and a laugh. He had better laugh because anything he says can and will be held against him in a story.

As I walked to the house, I noticed the beautiful peonies and irises along the fence that were planted years ago by his great aunts and how they bloom and offer a sweet fragrance each year, despite what trials or errors may come our way. Springtime on the farm is busy with calves being born, milk being hauled, and making hay while the sun shines, which gives us a lot of time together to work alongside each other or in spite of each other.

What a blessing!

MY JOURNAL

What made me laugh today

_____
_____
_____

What am I grateful for

_____
_____
_____
_____
_____

Bigger isn't always Better

You've heard all the sayings: "Bigger is better." "He who dies with the most toys wins." "The only difference between men and boys is the price of their toys." Blah, blah, blah. My boss finally got the big blue New Holland tractor he deserved, complete with air conditioning, heat, forward-reverse shuttle shift, enclosed cab, yada yada yada. He claims he bought it for me because I can reach the pedals. Next, he'll be trying to convince me to buy some swampland in Florida so that we can enjoy vacations together. But first, I must mention that we have had the tractor for several years, and I rarely drive it. But if buying it for me makes him feel good, then I'm going to roll with it and buy myself some more shoes for him.

I preferred to drive the Farmall 544 with none of the amenities except the gear pattern written in permanent marker on the loader bracket. It does have a radio, but to hear it, you must increase the volume to a point where the lyrics are unrecognizable. It does allow you to get a tan, farmer style, and smell the fragrance of honeysuckle and fresh-mowed hay. I'm a multitasker, and this tractor allows me to have a little pleasure while working.

The boss asked me to brush hog the remaining pastures after we finished hay, and I reluctantly agreed. That is how I usually succumb to working on the farm, reluctantly. He informed me that the brush hog was already hooked up to the New Holland. With that in mind, I had received a CRASH course in the morning, and that afternoon, I was to fly solo on HIS tractor.

Everything was quiet on the farm that warm afternoon as I climbed into the big blue tractor, trying to remember everything I was taught. I adjusted the seat to petite, checked all the controls, and somewhat confidently began to move forward. I was continually looking behind me to watch the brush hog to make sure it was working properly. I felt something dragging, but everything appeared to be in working order. So, I proceeded and figured an increase in throttle might solve the little dragging problem. Once I was sure everything behind me was working as planned, I turned around only to notice that the loader was not in the proper position. When I adjusted my seat, I accidentally hit the joystick, and now the loader was in "plowing position." The bucket was not on the loader; therefore, it made a nice double trench as I pushed it along the ground for several yards.

 I hit speed dial #2 on my cell phone, or 911 for a farmer's wife in trouble. I explained the situation to him and thought I might get points for diagnosing the problem myself. He was not impressed, nor did I get any bonus points. I couldn't even get fired. He was not seeing the 'joy' in the stick problem. I resumed the assigned task of driving this big blue tractor while brush hogging, with the air conditioning blowing hair in my face, unable to smell the flowers or even get a tan. I drove around in circles for 3 hours, anticipating the arrival of the boss and his discovery of my plow job.

I didn't anticipate that he would make me fill in the trenches with a shovel. I now have blisters, calluses, and a bad attitude. If only I had some tulip bulbs, this could have turned out to be a sweet-smelling mistake.

And just like that, the farm wife gets a cute little Kubota tractor, and again, he said he bought it so I could reach the pedals. I would have preferred an excuse like, "She looks good in orange," because pedals are not my problem, but I will settle for whatever justification is needed until he asks me for justification for the jewelry or shoes I bought, and then I can provide excuses until the cows come home.

Fresh air and farm life equal funny memories and sometimes flowers.

MY JOURNAL

What made me laugh today

_____
_____
_____

What am I grateful for

_____
_____
_____
_____
_____

Taste like Chicken

Raising chickens wasn't a job that was plotted on my career ladder; however, I agreed to the task, keeping in mind that the end results justify the means. Only once had I participated in the end results! And I don't mean cooking the chicken for dinner; the step right before purchasing the chicken from the grocer is what I am talking about.

Our neighbor, Sue, hatched chicks in her incubator for us, and then we kept them in our laundry room until those cute, fuzzy yellow creatures became not so cute. It was at that point they went to the barn and then later to the eggmobile or out to pasture. Some egg layers never made it to the promised land, like the dumb cluck I found one morning in the barn with the coffee can on her head. Can you imagine such an addiction for a chicken? Are you still wondering what an eggmobile is? Of course not—everyone has one rolling around their pasture, housing chickens that act as mobile insecticides and manure spreaders during the day and egg producers in their free-range time. This particular model of eggmobile was not as sturdy as some. Occasional heavy winds would cause it to move automatically. But on a typical day, it was towed behind a four-wheeler from one paddock to the next, behind the cows that were rotationally grazed on our farm. One sad day, I found it at the bottom of the hill with several chicken casualties.

Back to the results. This particular processing day, my organized husband prepared the butchering area, aka the children's swing set in the backyard. If you would like to know how you too can get more use out of your children's playsets, just give us a call. He nailed a killin' cone to a fence post, and we were in business. Are you asking what a killin' cone is? I know you've seen them anytime you have driven alongside some road construction. Take one of those bright orange cones, turn it upside down, shove a chicken in headfirst, and whala, with the mark of Zorro, you have a killin' cone in use.

It was my job to do the women's work: acquiring hot water, cold water, a sharp knife, and lots of freezer bags. That wasn't all; I showed up with our two daughters and rubber gloves for everyone. I could tell by the look on you-know-who's face that the gloves were not necessary. The girls were just there for looks because they had no intention of being active participants. Neither did I, the one and only time my father shared such an adventure with me. One daughter saw it as the disgusting project that it was, and the other daughter found it to be a science project, having Daddy dissect any and all inedible parts and learning about the unknown innards. Taco showed up for some treats, as he normally does. Nothing is as funny as a short, happy dog running around with chicken feet hanging out of his mouth.

It was hard work, but it put a lot of wholesome food in our freezer that tastes just like chicken, and for that, we are thankful. I understand that is what farming is all about.

MY JOURNAL

What made me laugh today
_____
_____
_____

What am I grateful for
_____
_____
_____
_____
_____

Fishing with my Father

Twice a year, my dad and his three siblings get together at Stockton Lake for the Redneck Reunion at Ruark Bluff West. These four weeks are spent camping, fishing, frying food, fellowship, and a few far-fetched fishing stories. Each sibling has their own RV, and the three men have very similar boats. I say that because each one thinks his is a little bit bigger and better. Sibling competition, I like to call it.

I affectionately refer to this as the "Redneck Reunion" not because my family fits the traditional stigma that is seen on television, they still have most of their teeth and no mullets, but because they put on no pretenses. They are who they are! They all have had successful careers and served our country. They all have had tough times and tragedy. They all have had or are fighting cancer. And they all know the meaning of living life with the love of family and friends.

While the parents are camping, the next generation visits off and on during the scheduled time in hopes that the date they come is the day of THE fish fry. This year, there were some sweet fourth-generation campers. And to think this all started years ago with my grandparents, who turned a Lay's Potato Chip truck into a camper because my grandpa was a carpenter who cherished time with his family and fishing.

This year, I was thrilled to have the time to park my RV between my aunt's and uncle's, and my dad's campsites. I joined them for breakfast and supper, and the time in between was spent not being productive. That's a  hard statement to make for a Type A, agenda-keeping, organizing, and time-management maniac. But here is what I've learned about the statement "that's time I will never get back." I've often grumbled it as I've stood in line at Walmart, traffic jams, or just waiting on something or somebody that doesn't seem to understand how precious MY time is and what it is worth. As I sat in the boat trolling around the lake waiting for fish to bite, I spent time with my dad. Time I will never get back! Because what I've also learned is that our time together on this earth is short, and regardless of whether the fish are biting or not, that's not the purpose of this time. The one that got away is always bigger than the one that's in the live well. It's not a fishing story if it's all true. I also learned that after 50-plus years of fishing with my dad, it's okay to talk in the boat... he really had me on that one. I got the idea that my dad is more aware of time than I am. He is happy just to drive the boat, cast my rod, and net my fish. You may be thinking that's not fishing on my part. Well, no, I'm not going to win any tournaments that way or get my name on a big board with the 'catch of the day,' but I may get an ice cream from the marina if the boat needs gas. More importantly, I get memories. Memories of time well spent having conversations, laughing at my uncles that try to steal our fishing spot or lucky lure, time spent outdoors breathing in fresh air, soaking up some sun, relaxing, and reeling in life at a slower pace.

A few more things I've learned from the Redneck Reunion are that providing my uncles with baked treats ensures me hugs and a reprieve from fish cleaning. Paper plates, a few sticks of wood, and some gasoline make for a good fire and recycling. If duct tape won't fix it, then it's time to get something bigger and better. I've also learned that some family secrets are better left kept.

I am happy to say that this family tradition was shared with my girls and their friends and is one of the best vacation memories in the books. I think I've convinced the boss that this happy camper is worth all the 'glamping' he can provide. What a catch I got.

MY JOURNAL

What made me laugh today
_____
_____
_____

What am I grateful for
_____
_____
_____
_____
_____
_____

Fishing with My Father, Part 2: It's all about the Bling

I used to think "It's all about the bling" was in reference to rhinestone-studded jeans, jackets, t-shirts, big flashy earrings, and bangle bracelets. But after fishing with my father, I've learned it's about the lures.

Photo Credit To Aunt Sissy

Fishing lure: a type of artificial fishing bait designed to attract a fish's attention. The lure uses movement, vibration, flash, and color to bait fish. While sitting in the boat on a hot summer day with my dad this year, I contemplated this definition. I was occasionally catching a fish when I noticed my dad was occasionally reeling in his line and changing his lure. I thought lures are like jewelry. First of all, you can never have enough. Some are universal and go with everything, yet some are for more specific uses or outfits, so one of every color, size, and style is needed. All range in price, with no guarantee to provide a good catch. My dad has multiple bling boxes in his boat. Actually, they are small plastic boxes with dividers that stack nicely and are organized very neatly. Every lure has a special hook to keep it and the fish from getting lost once hooked. Just like your favorite bracelet or necklace. While fishing, he would have a few of his favorite 'go-to' pieces laying out in the boat, but occasionally he'd have to resort to the box after conversing with my uncles about what is 'attractive' to the fish and what they were 'biting on.' Isn't that why we wear jewelry, to attract attention?

As a kid, I was never allowed to play with the lures. I always thought it was because of the hooks and the chance of getting hurt. I've witnessed a few times that my dad and uncles have gotten hurt doing just that: a hook in the eyebrow from a nearby cast or hooking thumbs together from trying to untangle lures. I've never had such an injury from a tangled necklace, so I think I'll stick with the jewelry. I did overhear my dad say, when referring to the number of lures in his boxes, "A lot of those, I didn't even know I had." Once again, just like jewelry. I might mention that quality, quantity, and cost are also family secrets. That refers to both fishing lures and jewelry.

When I inquired about why none of the lures looked like actual fish, my cousin informed me that it was because they don't have to look like the fish, just attract them. Oh, I get it! Kind of like cubic zirconia and diamonds. They don't have to be the real bling thing, just be shiny and eye-catching. Which brings me to a little trivia: Did you know that the 1853 copper Gian Haskell Minnow is likely the most expensive production lure ever sold? When the bidding ended in 2003 at a whopping amount of $101,200, this lure became the highest-priced fishing-related collectible sold at an auction. It's not the Hope diamond, but it puts 'costume' jewelry into perspective.

More thoughts... I don't know what the average lure costs. With a tiny clasp, one hooks this lure on a thin piece of line connected to a long stick with a reel on it and then throws it into a large body of water filled with logs, trees, a few fish, and other obstacles that could be snagged along with "the one that got away." I have lost a sentimental piece of jewelry before, and it made me incredibly sad. Do you think that happens when you lose a lure? I know my dad and uncles will spend a lot of time avoiding the dreaded "cut the line" solution. Makes me think they are worth more than just a few bucks.

Next time you go fishing and are figuring out what to wear, how to dress, or how to bait, here are two things I learned from my dad and my uncles: 1. Red sky at night, sailor's delight; red sky in the morning, sailor's take warning. (Check this out in the Bible, it's actually a true fish story: Matthew 16:2-3). 2. Winds blowing from the west, fish bite the best. Winds blowing from the east, fish bite the least. (No reference to truth in this statement.)

My father's tackle boxes, just like my jewelry box, are full of things that sparkle, dangle, a little tarnished with time and exposure, but there is my favorite 'lure' that is sparkly and fits my finger well, that always reminds me I got the catch of the day, 28 years ago. The best fishing story ever, a bit embellished but mostly true.

MY JOURNAL

What made me laugh today

_____
_____
_____

What am I grateful for

_____
_____
_____
_____
_____
_____

The Final Cast

The annual Redneck Reunion at Stockton Lake has dwindled to two brothers and their boats. The days of ghost stories and donuts made out of canned biscuits have faded. Children grow up and have children of their own. Schedules get busy, and family members pass on to the best fishing spot, where waters never end.

The last few years, I have been blessed to have a husband who will take me and my big ole camper to the lake, leave me, and come home to work while I fish with my father and create a few more memories this side of heaven.

The annual camping trips are always during the busiest seasons on the farm, and I always feel a bit guilty for leaving the ranch work for a life of leisure. But I know these camping trips are limited in quantity and treasures I'll never regret.

Camping these days, there is a bit less time fishing and more resting. Although my father and his brother both have a boat, they never fish together. Well, then they'd have to reveal their secret lures. Yet, they always know where on the lake the other one is fishing and have some idea if they are having any luck reeling in the big ones.

On a typical day, I was blessed if my dad and his brother stopped by my camper for a cup of coffee each morning, followed by breakfast, which still consists of quail, biscuits and gravy, a short respite, then some fishing, followed by an afternoon nap, and if I was lucky, a supper meal of fried fish and french fries. Pies were required as a payment to my uncle to keep me from having to clean fish. Time around the campfire now ends at sundown, and everyone returns to their camper to watch the news and retire for the evening before starting all over again the next day.

Both my dad and his brother have the same type of cancer. They receive the same treatment on the same days at the same location and choose this as a day to confuse nurses with their same first initial and last name, a trick that also caused chaos in their 20+ year military careers—but to also have lunch and discuss the next fishing trip. As the cancer has progressed, my dad's treatment has intensified. He's always known that there was no cure for his type of cancer, and he's always said that it was a tool to connect him to other people dealing with the disease. This allowed him to be a fisher of men and share about God's saving grace and hope.

Determination to live life to the fullest has kicked in, and these brothers continue to embrace what they love the most: fishing and family. The stories get more elaborate the more they are repeated, the hugs get longer, and the sunsets more beautiful.

As I write this last fishing-with-my-father story, my dad is casting in the clouds with the one who can fill his net abundantly and heal his body completely. Time on the lake, fishing with my father—that's time I'll never get back, and I'm glad it was well spent.

MY JOURNAL

What made me laugh today
_____
_____
_____

What am I grateful for
_____
_____
_____
_____
_____
_____

Cruisin' on the Buffalo River

I've seen buffalo and I've cruised on ships, but never have I experienced cruising like I did on the Buffalo River. The Martins and the Wormingtons were spending a relaxing weekend in Arkansas in a cozy cabin tucked back in the woods. Yes, the music from Deliverance could be heard if one listened closely.

It was a chilly but beautiful day when my husband sent my best friend and me down the river in a canoe.

He thought it best that we go together and leave the children to float with a responsible adult—he and my dad. That's when the adventure began. You see, we didn't know our aft from a hole in the ground filled with water. We were even curious about the purpose of the rope trailing from the front of the canoe. It wasn't long before we discovered it was for pulling us out of a sinking predicament. There is no sound like the yelling of two Type A, strong-willed women in a canoe. I might add, we are both directionally challenged, but that's not a problem when everything floats downstream. Neither of us knew what we were doing, but you can be sure we acted like we did. Our only experience in a canoe had been looking pretty. That's what our men tell us to do when they don't want us actively participating in paddling while they are in the boat with us. On this day, we were failing at that, too; there was nothing pretty about the situations we found ourselves in or the words we used to get us out.

We tried to find the beauty in the adventure, but every time we looked up, we saw what lay ahead and panicked. The figurehead, a nautical term for a woman carved in the front of a ship, would start yelling at the stern one, i.e., the one with the paddles doing all the work. Then, if things didn't go her way, she would jump ship, get out of the canoe. Well, as the saying goes, the captain goes down with the ship; it was clear I was not the first mate.

It was only about 15 minutes into the journey that we managed to start taking on some water. Frustration had already consumed us when the figurehead yelled, "Let it go!" I wasn't sure if she meant the concept of a successful sail or the canoe. So, not wanting to give in to defeat, I let go of the canoe because she had already jumped ship. Yes, downstream it went, no paddling necessary. Can you hear the music from the movie Frozen? It wasn't long before I caught the glare of my husband, who waited in the water as my canoe headed straight for him. I knew the glare, and it was not a term of endearment that he was thinking. He caught the canoe and brought it back to us. Ahhhh, that is the purpose of the rope. We crawled back in, just as mad as two wet hens could be.

Things seemed to be going a little smoother when we noticed a lot of brightly colored rocks at the bottom of the river. Coincidentally, they were the colors of canoes. Soon, we were stuck again!

By the end of the day and the end of this journey, we were all but speechless. Not exactly, but our vocal cords needed a rest. Our clothes were wet, our attitudes were damp, and our friendship was drowning. It was the other floaters, who had overheard the day's conversations, that cheered us on as we dragged our ship from the raging waters of the Buffalo. Perhaps the waters weren't raging; it was just our personalities.

Our friendship is still intact, unlike the canoe. We still cruise together, but on much bigger ships and with a trained professional at the helm.

MY JOURNAL

What made me laugh today

_____
_____
_____

What am I grateful for

_____
_____
_____
_____
_____
_____

Joy to the world, the Lord

Joy to the world, the Lord is come

Let Earth receive her King

Let every heart prepare Him room

And Heaven and nature sing…

Before the angels appeared to the shepherds on the hillside, there had been 400 years of silence. Between the pages of the Old Testament and the New, a mere second for us to flip a page, lived a people group waiting in anticipation of their Messiah. During those 400 years, there had been no new word from God or prophets, no revelations, no signs. I suspect the Israelites got used to the silence and somehow made peace with the longing in waiting or despair of being rescued, accepting it as the 'new normal,' as we like to call things in our world today. I know that sometimes we get comfortable with what was once uncomfortable because we are not willing to make a change. Change is hard. Farming is ever-changing if the goal is sustainability.  Sometimes it means doing things that have never been done in many generations of farming and trusting that it will work, not based on experience, but rather on faith.

The shepherds who set out with their flocks, more than likely the sheep that would be used as the sacrificial lamb at the Passover meal that day, were preoccupied with their work. I doubt they had any idea this was the day the Messiah was coming; it was probably just another day at the office. Imagine the angels appearing. That would be a divine interruption! I sometimes wonder if God sent us a sign like that today—angels in the sky or a bright star—would we notice? There's a good chance we'd be looking down at our phones or to-do lists and miss it.

I wonder, like the Israelites, if sometimes we lose our sense of eager anticipation for Jesus to return to us. Have we become so accustomed to filling the void in our souls with worldly things in the waiting that we have forgotten He is the only one who can truly satisfy? There is a difference between moments of happiness and uncontrollable joy. A chocolate donut and a cup of coffee can make me happy, but once they are gone and I realize I didn't really need to eat that for my health, the happiness fades.

'Tis the season of Christmas. A time when we should celebrate the first coming and look forward to the second coming, but yet we get so busy and give all our attention to the now. But in all the preparations, I don't want to neglect preparing my heart. Sometimes, I read a 'Christmas'-themed book like Can Martha Have a Mary Christmas by Brenda Poinsett, or Skipping Christmas by John Grisham, or the book of Luke in the Bible. But none of this equates to being still and aware of God's presence in my life every day. Being still seems like such a foreign concept during this season, when there are gifts to be bought and wrapped, decorating to be done, lists to be made, food to be prepared, and on and on and on. Once again, we are looking for the approval of others to fill our souls instead of the One who truly can. I know there is so much more that God wants to share with me and show me than twinkling lights, pretty packages, and Christmas songs. It seems so strange that the busiest season of all is the one where we should be still and ponder. This busy is the thing that steals our time and presence.

Walking alongside someone and helping to carry their burden, what a gift to give. Sitting quietly and listening to someone tell their story, the gift of time. Taking someone a meal, a gift of compassion or talent, if cooking is your gift. But if we are too busy to notice the burdens and needs of others, we miss the opportunity to give. So, with any season, my goal is to be still and know. Sometimes being still mentally is more of a challenge because the list of things I want to do is long and the days are short. As the saying goes, if we think it is important, we will make time; otherwise, we will make an excuse.

So, this season, I want to give Jesus my best present, my presence.

MY JOURNAL

What made me laugh today
_____
_____
_____

What am I grateful for
_____
_____
_____
_____
_____
_____

Made in the USA
Coppell, TX
20 January 2026

68717368R00105